BETWEEN HELL AND HEAVEN

K.G. HARSHAA

Made with ♥ on the Notion Press Platform
www.notionpress.com

<u>**To my Father and Mother**</u>

Your unwavering belief in me has been the foundation of this book. Your support has given me strength, confidence, and courage to share my story.

This journey is as much yours as it is mine.

Contents

FOREWORD

Blade "The Blade" Hunter isn't your typical hero. He's the guy you call when your problems are too messy for anyone else to handle. Because, he's not picky about who's right or wrong; all that matters to him is eliminating the problem, getting paid and staying alive. Whether it's taking out the worst of the worst or the so-called good guys, its all the same for him. His loyal companion, Buster, is always vigilent, ready to protect him when things spiral out of control. Strap in for a chaotic ride full of bullets, bad decisions, and a lot of sarcasm.

Preface

This story started with a simple question:
What if the world was a little more chaotic, and the person trying to survive it was a bit less heroic?

I wanted to create a character who didn't play by the rules, someone who wasn't bogged down by moral dilemmas or deep introspection. This character became a mercenary - doing a job that pays well, cracking jokes in the middle of danger, and riding the rollercoaster of chaos where the only thing that matters is surviving the next day.

If you're ready for a ride packed with humor, danger, and some seriously questionable decisions, then you're in the right spot.

Acknowledgements

I would like to express my heartfelt gratitude to everyone who has supported me on this incredible journey of creating Between Hell and Heaven. Your encouragement and belief in me has been invaluable.

A special thanks to my family for their endless love and unwavering support, and especially to my sister for her insightful and constructive feedback, which has helped to make this book even more engaging.

I would also like to express my sincere gratitude to all the readers of my previous book, A Bat and A Ball. Your support and thoughtful feedback was truly inspiring and encouraged me to grow as a writer and refine my storytelling.

Finally, I would like to acknowledge the support of my publishing team for their efforts in bringing this book to readers.

Thank you all for being part of this journey!

PROLOGUE

So, who is this Mercenary?

The city sprawled out like a restless beast under a heavy blanket of night. Rain drizzled incessantly, each drop a tiny hammer striking the cracked pavement, creating a symphony of whispers in the dark. The streets, slick with the sheen of the wetness, gleamed under the pale glow of flickering streetlights, casting long, distorted shadows that danced and writhed like phantom figures.

The air was thick with the scent of damp earth and distant smoke, a haunting reminder of the city's ceaseless hunger for destruction and rebirth. Alleyways twisted and turned like the intestines of some great, slumbering monster, filled with secrets and echoes of lives lost to the darkness.

In the heart of this urban labyrinth stood an abandoned warehouse, its looming silhouette etched against the horizon like a jagged scar. The building, with its boarded-up windows and rusted corrugated iron, seemed to breathe in tandem with the city, exhaling an air of foreboding. Ivy crept up its walls, as if nature itself were trying to reclaim this forsaken structure.

Inside, the warehouse was a cavern of shadows, illuminated only by the occasional shaft of moonlight that pierced through the cracks in the roof. The air was stagnant, heavy with dust and the metallic tang of old machinery. Cobwebs hung like tattered curtains, swaying gently in an unseen breeze, and the floor was littered with the remnants of a forgotten past – broken crates, rusted tools, and the occasional rat scurrying into the darkness.

This was a place where dreams came to die, where the weight of despair pressed down on the shoulders of those foolish enough to seek refuge within its walls. It was here that Blake "The Blade" Hunter would make his stand, caught in the crossfire between heaven and hell, the very fabric of his existence stretched thin.

As the first drops of rain began to fall, Blake stood at the precipice of his destiny, a solitary figure in a world of shades and shadows. The storm was coming, and with it, the promise of chaos and revelation.

"Hey folks, this is me Blake, the merciless mercenary who has quite questionable doubts! I have one for you, ever had one of those days where you can't decide whether you're a hero or a villain? No? Just me, then? Well, sit tight, because this is a tale of chaos, contradiction, and the absolute lunacy of walking the line between heaven and hell.

Hey, bub, introduce me to them. They look uncomfortable, I'm not a bad guy, just a... You know what, I'm a baddie!"

Meet Blake "The Blade" Hunter – assassin-for-hire, mercenary extraordinaire, and the guy your favorite antihero calls when they need a job done, no questions asked.

You got a problem? He's got a solution, and it usually involves a lot of bullets and a healthy disregard for the rules. Good guys, bad guys – he's worked for them all. Because in this line of work, morality is as gray as the concrete jungles he prowls.

So, what happens when Blake gets contracted by both sides of the ethical spectrum at the same time? The good guys want him to take out the worst of the bad, a villain with a heart blacker than midnight. The bad guys, on the other hand, have a target who's so squeaky clean you'd think they showered in holy water.

Here's the kicker – both targets are each other. Yep, a classic standoff. Our anti-hero is stuck in the middle of an existential tug-of-war, armed with nothing but his sarcasm, a loaded gun, and a moral compass that's been spinning for years.

Ryan Reynolds, the merch with the mouth, would nail the role – his sharp wit and devil-may-care attitude bringing Blake to life in technicolor sarcasm, however that would never happen for sure. As the story unfolds, expect bullet-strewn action scenes, quippy one-liners, and a deep dive into the psyche of a man who's made his home in the gray areas of right and wrong and many fourth walls will be broken.

I

THE PHANTOM'S SHADOW

Alright, here we go again. Another day, another dollar, another morally ambiguous contract. You know the drill. But this time, it's big – like 'I should probably reconsider my life choices' big.

Meet The Phantom, my next paycheck – and no, I'm not talking about the cool comic book character. This guy's a real piece of work. Corruption, scams, violence – you name it, he's done it. If there's a shady deal going down in this city, you can bet The Phantom's fingerprints are all over it. I've worked for him in a case to kill people. That catty imbecile, who will 'die alone', did this as if I get caught, he won't get the blame.

So, what's a guy like me doing, taking a job like this? Easy. The pay is enough to make even a cynical, jaded mercenary like me consider early retirement. Not that I'd know what to do with all that free time. Maybe take up knitting. Yeah, Blake the Knitter. That's got a nice ring to it.

Anyway, back to the task at hand. The Phantom's headquarters is a fortress. Seriously, this place makes Fort Knox look like a sandbox. Armed guards, security cameras, booby traps – the works. But hey, when has that ever stopped me?

Let's break it down, shall we? We're about to take on this Phantom guy, the city's top dog of criminal mischief. And speaking of dogs, meet my partner in crime or murder – Buster. Yeah, that's right, Buster. Not the most intimidating name, but don't let it fool you. This dog is sharper than most people I know. Aren't you, Buster?"

Buster, a scrappy little mutt with a face only a mother could love, wagged his tail enthusiastically. His beady eyes sparkled with mischief, and there was something almost human in his expression, as if he understood every word Blake said.

"Now, Buster here might look like a walking flea circus, but he's got a nose for trouble – literally. This little furball can sniff out a lie faster than you can say 'bad guy.' And trust me, in this line of work, that's a handy skill to have."

Blake unfolded a crumpled piece of paper and laid it out on the table. It was a blueprint of The Phantom's Fortress. "Here's the plan," he said, tapping the paper with a gloved finger. "We sneak in through the back, where security is weakest. There's a vent here," he pointed, "that leads straight into the heart of the compound. From there, we make our way to the control room, disable the cameras, and then it's a straight shot to The Phantom's lair. Next, we pop a bullet into his damn forehead!"

Buster barked in agreement, or maybe he just liked the sound of Blake's voice. It was hard to tell sometimes.

"Good boy, Buster. Now, you're gonna keep an eye out while I do my thing. If anything goes sideways, you know the drill – distract and disable. And by disable, I mean that adorable face of yours should convince anyone to let down their guard. Works every time."

Buster nodded – or at least it seemed like he did. Blake couldn't help but chuckle. "Who's a good boy? You are, Buster. You're the best sidekick a morally ambiguous mercenary could ask for."

Blake paused for a moment, staring at the blueprints. "Wait, why am I doing this?" he asked aloud. "Oh right, the money! I do this for the money, as I am risking my life and Buster's too. Otherwise, I don't give a damn about these guys! If my job were to be partners, I would be! But there's no time for changing sides!"

He chuckled, and started blabbering "You remember Casablanca, Buster? 'Of all the gin joints in all the towns in all the world, she walks into mine.' Well, buddy, of all the contracts in all the cities in all the world, we gotta take this one. Here's lookin' at you, kid."

With the plan set, Blake geared up, checking his weapons and tools. Buster trotted by his side, a picture of canine loyalty and determination. Together, they were an unlikely duo, but they'd seen each other through countless missions and survived more close calls than Blake cared to count.

I bet you've been wondering, why on earth are they paying money for him to do this. Well, while his plan may be simple, not a single job has this merc ever failed to complete. Killing loads of people? Yes. Take on the city's biggest criminals? Yes. Kill a bunch of poor citizens just for the money? I might be ashamed but, yes... Remember, I told ya, "Every hero starts as a villain, becomes an anti-hero and finally, becomes a hero" or did I? I don't remember, but do you care? Probably not. So, let's get into action!

Blake and Buster hailed a taxi, blending into the city's nightscape. The cab's interior smelled of worn leather and faint traces of cologne – a mix of professionalism and countless stories from countless fares.

Blake sank into the back seat, Buster hopping up next to him, his paws on Blake's knee, eagerly looking out the window. "Evening, buddy," Blake greeted the driver, a grizzled man with deep lines etched into his face, each one perhaps a testament to the lives he had driven around this sprawling metropolis.

"Where to?" the driver asked, his voice a gravelly murmur.

"Take us to the old industrial district, and step on it, if you don't mind," Blake replied, glancing at Buster. "We've got a murder to do."

The driver arched an eyebrow, glancing at Buster. "I hope you aren't serious. Your dog got a name?"

"Buster," Blake said, leaning back. "If he starts singing, don't be surprised. We were just kiddin'", Blake played himself, knowing that this driver was one of those 'good' people' who would definitely go to heaven.

"Right," the driver chuckled. "Any special occasion?"

"Yeah, we're on our way to take down a crime lord," Blake said casually. "You know, usual Tuesday night stuff."

The driver snorted, clearly thinking it was a joke. "What kind of crime lord?"

"The Phantom," Blake said, emphasizing the name with dramatic flair. "Sounds like a bad guy from a 90s action movie, doesn't it?"

"Sure does," the driver agreed, shaking his head with amusement. "Good luck with that, buddy."

As the taxi weaved through the city streets, Blake glanced at the driver's collection of bobbleheads on the dashboard. "Nice collection," he remarked. "You got Batman, Iron Man, and... is that a Darth Vader holding a bouquet of roses?"

The driver grinned. "Yeah, got that one from a street fair. Pretty unique, huh?"

"Definitely unique," Blake said with a chuckle. "You should see Buster's collection of chew toys. He's got a Chewbacca, a Groot, and even a mini-Hulk."

Buster barked in agreement, his eyes wide with excitement.

The driver cast a curious glance in the rearview mirror. "You know, you two make quite the pair. Ever thought about starting a podcast or something?"

"Funny you should say that" Blake said. "We've thought about it, but we're too busy saving the world, one contract at a time."

They arrived at the edge of the industrial district, a desolate expanse of crumbling warehouses and rusted machinery. The taxi pulled to a stop outside a seemingly abandoned building, its windows dark and foreboding.

"This is it," Blake said, handing over the fare with a generous tip. "Thanks for the ride."

"Good luck, Batman and Robin," the driver replied with a wink.

Blake stepped out, Buster at his side. The night air was thick with the scent of oil and decay, a fitting prelude to the mission ahead.

As they approached The Phantom's fortress, Blake glanced down at Buster. "Ready, partner?"

Buster barked once, as if to say, "Born ready."

Blake smirked. "Alright, let's do this. It's all about strategic planning and precision, buddy. Think about it like we're in 'Mission: Impossible.' No, really. Imagine Tom

Cruise hanging from the ceiling. Now, imagine I'm better looking and without the crazy stunts – but with a solid plan."

Blake explained his approach with a mix of humor and advanced concepts. "First, let's tackle that vent. We need to use fluid dynamics to calculate the optimal flow of air and temperature differentials. Bernoulli's principle tells us that as the velocity of a fluid increases, the pressure within the fluid decreases. So, we adjust our entry speed to minimize noise and avoid triggering pressure-sensitive alarms."

Buster tilted his head, seemingly trying to follow along.

"Next up, we'll navigate the ventilation system. It's all about minimizing resonance. Resonance frequencies can amplify vibrations, making our movements detectable. By calculating the natural frequency of the vent system and moving in a way that avoids those frequencies, we stay stealthy. Simple harmonic motion principles, really. Think of it like walking to the beat of an invisible drummer."

Blake carefully made his way through the vents, Buster following closely. "Now, for the control room, we'll use a bit of advanced electromagnetism. Remember 'The Matrix'? It's kind of like that. We'll create a localized electromagnetic field to induce a voltage spike in the camera circuits, effectively short-circuiting them without a full EMP burst."

Reaching the control room, Blake pulled out a compact device. "This little beauty here is an electromagnetic pulse emitter. Not the kind that takes out an entire city block – just enough to scramble their electronics. We need to calculate the exact electromagnetic field strength to avoid collateral damage. Maxwell's equations should help us here."

With the push of a button, the cameras went dark. Blake grinned, "The Phantom's lair is right down the hall. We take him out, collect our paycheck, and then maybe I'll teach you how to play poker."

Blake and Buster approached the final door. "Remember, Buster," Blake whispered, "it's all about timing and precision. Just like 'Inception.' We layer our actions perfectly to pull off the heist. Let's finish this."

As they reached the final room, Blake checked his watch. "Now, if my calculations are correct, The Phantom should be right behind this door." He glanced at Buster. "Ready for some action, partner?"

Buster wagged his tail in affirmation.

Blake took a deep breath and kicked open the door, ready to confront The Phantom. The room was dark, except for the dim glow of a single lamp. The Phantom stood at the center, a sinister smile playing on his lips.

Blake raised his weapon, his voice steady. "Game over, Phantom."

"Oh yeah, is it? And who in The Matrix are you?" The Phantom asked, standing tall, smirking in the way which felt a bit suspicious.

"Oh, you're a fan too! Nice!" Blake cried hysterically. Then, he turned away, and...

"Hey! So, this is the guy who I told! The big criminal mastermind who has an entire company of I don't know, baby diapers? And I am gonna pop a nice full metal Jacket from my dazzling M16 rifle and... Oh, shucks!" Blake cried.

Blake, you dimwit! Stick to the script, you fumbling idiot! It's not baby diapers, it's gun manufacturing!

"Cut the cackle, you imbecile! The script tells me to forget my M16, and only bring my bullets as a way of... You know, dark humor or some stuff I don't care! And the company doesn't matter, he's gonna die anyway!"

Oh, that's dark. Go on, Blake! Audience, this guy needs some serious therapy...

"What the hell are you doing here, Blake? Why are the lights off?" The Phantom shouted, brandishing his gun.

"Can I have one? Holy smokes, is that a Wilson Combat SFX9 Pistol? Te daré una bala, dame el arma, tonto", Blake asked. If Buster had a voice, this book would be rated 16+. That was the stupidest question ever (and the worst Spanish too).

Wasn't it, Buster? Oh! Such a cutie!

They were trapped. This was over, and Blake was going to fail his first... But remember, The Phantom's smile was suspicious.

There was initially a gentle tap on the door, which gradually intensified into loud bangs. Blake concluded that an individual was persistently knocking on the door.

"Open up, Phantom! You instructed us to be here within ten minutes!" a voice rang out, sounding both forceful and soft.

Subsequently, the door was opened with a resounding noise, revealing several individuals armed with knives. They looked ripped too!

"He's low budget too! Phantom, why won't you give them proper..." Blake's question was cut off by...

"Finish him! Drat this gun, it's out of bullets! I have other matters to attend to!" The Phantom snarled, tossing the empty firearm aside. He walked out of the room with an air of indifference, whistling a haunting tune. Blake's face contorted with frustration, and for the first time, Buster felt the cold grip of fear. The loyal dog had never experienced such a chilling sensation until this moment, even with his unwavering bond to his owner.

Blake looked down at Buster, who was trembling. "We're in deep trouble, buddy. If we don't make it out of this, know that I'm proud of you, and don't look into my closet, if you're alive!" Blake murmured, his voice heavy with resignation.

As Buster attempted to escape, Blake grabbed hold of him, but they were quickly surrounded by the menacing gym rats. The thugs, with their muscular frames and sinister grins, closed in, their presence suffocating. The sight of their grotesque faces sent a wave of terror through Buster.

Blake straightened up, his eyes blazing with defiance. "Alright, you guys want a fight to the death? It's going to get messy. Blood will be spilled, so look away if you're squeamish! It's gonna be gore, okay?" He glanced at Buster, his voice softening for a brief moment.

"Righto! Buster, this isn't going to be pretty. But you were raised by me, and I know you have the heart of a warrior. Do what you need to do to survive."

You're dead meat, Blake...

Blake took a deep breath, his mind racing with the chaos that was about to unfold. He glanced down at Buster, who seemed equally confused but ready for anything. "Alright, Buster," Blake whispered, "showtime. Let's give them a performance they'll forget, as they'll die anyway!"

The crooks closed in; their faces twisted into sneers. Blake's heart pounded, but he couldn't resist the urge to throw in a little banter. "Nice invisible guns, fellas. Did you get those in a two-for-one sale? Because it looks like you forgot to load them!"

The first thug lunged forward, brandishing a knife. Blake sidestepped smoothly, his movements almost dance-like. "Ever seen a tango with knives? No? Well, you're in for a treat!" With a swift motion, Blake disarmed the thug, sending the knife clattering to the floor.

Another goon aimed a punch at Blake's head, but he ducked just in time. "Really? You guys need to work on your coordination. This is starting to feel like an episode of a slapstick comedy."

Buster, not to be left out, seized the opportunity. He darted between the thugs' legs, barking ferociously. One of the crooks, startled by the furry menace, tripped over his own feet, and landed in a heap.

Blake couldn't help but laugh. "Buster, my man! You've got the moves of a ninja. Or maybe just a really confused squirrel, but it's working!"

Blake grabbed a nearby pipe, twirling it like a baton. "Let's add some physics to the mix, shall we? Conservation of momentum, anyone?" He swung the pipe, knocking out two thugs with a single blow. "Kinetic energy transferred efficiently. Just like I planned!"

Another goon tried to grab Blake from behind, but Buster intervened, biting the thug's ankle. The man yelped in pain, hopping around on one foot. "Buster, that's not just a bite – that's a tactical maneuver. I'll have to give you a treat for that one!"

Blake spun around, using the distraction to his advantage. He elbowed the thug in the face, sending him sprawling. "They should really put up a sign – 'Beware of Dog.'"

The remaining crooks hesitated, clearly rethinking their life choices. Blake, ever the showman, saw his moment to shine. "Alright, boys, let's wrap this up. It's been fun, but I've got a guy to kill and money to get!"

With a final flurry of punches and kicks, Blake took down the last of the goons. He stood amidst the chaos, breathing heavily but grinning ear to ear. "Well, that was invigorating. Who needs a gym membership when you've got this kind of workout?"

Buster trotted over, wagging his tail proudly. Blake knelt down, scratching behind the dog's ears. "You did good, buddy. We make a pretty good team, don't we?"

Blake looked around at the unconscious thugs, shaking his head in amusement. "They never learn, do they? But hey, at least we got our cardio in for the day."

He straightened up, ready to pursue The Phantom. "Alright, partner, let's go finish this. We've got a criminal mastermind to catch, and I've got a feeling he's not going to make it easy."

Buster barked in agreement, and together they charged out of the room, ready for whatever came next.

Blake stood amidst the chaos, his senses heightened and adrenaline pumping. One of the thugs, a brawly guy, decided to try his luck. With a menacing grin, he pulled out a gleaming knife and hurled it straight at Blake.

Blake's reflexes kicked in, and he dodged the knife with a fluid motion. "Oh, nice try, buddy!" he called out, his voice dripping with sarcasm. "But let me show you how it's done."

In one swift movement, Blake snatched the knife from the air, spun it around in his hand, and with pinpoint accuracy, threw it back at the thug. The knife sailed through the air, embedding itself right in the thug's chest.

The thug's eyes widened in shock as he staggered backward, clutching at the knife. Blake couldn't resist a quip. "I should have gone for the head," he muttered, shaking his head in mock disappointment.

Buster barked in approval, his tail wagging furiously. Blake glanced down at his furry companion. "What do you think, Buster? Should I start giving knife-throwing lessons?

It might be a nice side gig."

The thug collapsed to the ground, and Blake turned his attention back to the remaining goons. "Alright, who's next? Anyone else want to try their luck?"

The other thugs hesitated, clearly rethinking their life choices. Blake smirked, ready for whatever came next. "Come on, fellas. Let's make this interesting."

Blake and Buster charged down the dimly lit corridor, the sound of their footsteps echoing off the walls. The Phantom's lair was just ahead, and Blake could feel the adrenaline coursing through his veins. He glanced down at Buster, who was trotting beside him, eyes sharp and focused.

"Alright, buddy," Blake whispered. "This is it. Time to take down The Phantom."

They reached the heavy metal door at the end of the hall. Blake took a deep breath and kicked it open, bursting into the room with his gun raised. The Phantom stood at the center, a sinister smile playing on his lips.

"Ah, Blake," The Phantom sneered. "I was wondering when you'd show up."

Blake didn't waste any time. He fired a warning shot, the bullet whizzing past The Phantom's ear. "Game over, Phantom. You're done."

The Phantom laughed, a cold, mirthless sound. "You think you can just walk in here and take me down? You're more foolish than I thought."

Blake's eyes narrowed. "I've taken down worse than you. And I've got a secret weapon." He glanced at Buster, who barked in agreement.

The Phantom's smile faltered. "A dog? You think a dog can stop me?"

Blake smirked. "This isn't just any dog. Buster, now!"

Buster sprang into action, darting towards The Phantom with surprising speed. The Phantom tried to react, but Buster was too quick. He leaped up, sinking his teeth into The Phantom's arm, causing him to drop his weapon.

Blake seized the opportunity. He lunged forward, delivering a swift punch to The Phantom's jaw, sending him sprawling to the ground. "That's for all the lives you've ruined, or just mine!" Blake growled.

The Phantom struggled to get up, but Blake was already on him. He pressed the barrel of his gun to The Phantom's forehead. "Any last words?"

The Phantom's eyes were filled with fear. "You... you can't do this. You're supposed to be my loyal worker. We can make a deal!"

Blake's expression hardened. "First of all, the only deal I'm interested in is seeing you six feet under. Consider it closed. Second of all, I'm nobody's quote, unquote, loyal worker. I'm just the guy who gets the job done, gets the money, enjoys the rest of his life. Third of all, I didn't shoot your thugs, as I want to enjoy killing you, and you should thank me for that! Fifth... Or is it fourth, it doesn't matter coz I don't care!" He pulled the trigger, and The Phantom's body went limp.

With that, Blake pulled the trigger. The Phantom's body went limp as the bullet pierced through him. Blake shot him six times. BASH! BASH! BASH! Each shot echoed through the warehouse, a symphony of finality.

Blake stood up, breathing heavily. He looked down at Buster, who was wagging his tail proudly. "Well, that was a lead overdose. Guess I'm just an overachiever. Good job, buddy. We did it. Now, time to remove all the possible evidence! Just got to clean all the damn blood. Damn it!"

After thoroughly cleaning all his marks and potential traces, he glanced around the 'now clean' room after taking in the chaos. "Let's get out of here. We've got a paycheck to collect."

As they left The Phantom's lair, Blake couldn't help but feel a sense of satisfaction. It wasn't about being a hero or a villain. It was about doing what needed to be done. No loyalty, no sense of evilness... nor goodness. Just cash. Or money.

Blake and Buster exited The Phantom's lair, the weight of their actions settling in. As they walked down the empty street, Blake's phone rang. He glanced at the screen and answered.

"Blake, what happened to The Phantom? He still isn't here!" a tense voice demanded.

Blake hesitated, then replied with a grin, "Oh, you know, just a little case of severe 'ouch-my-everything'."

The voice on the other end grew more urgent. "Severe 'ouch-my-everything'? What do you mean?"

"He died," Blake said nonchalantly.

A pause. "No! You could have brought him to the hospital!"

Blake's grin widened. "I don't think a hospital can fix a terminal case of villainy."

"But what about his cancer? What were his last words?"

Blake's eyes sparkled with mischief as he recalled the confrontation. "He told me, 'You can't do this.'"

"So, what did you do?" the voice pressed.

Blake chuckled. "Well, when life gives you lemons, you squeeze them right back into life's face. So, I did."

The voice grew frantic. "How did he die? How did you eliminate him?"

Blake's voice was cheerful. "He died because I helped him reach his 'full potential'—six feet under. With a side of creative flair, if I do say so myself!"

A stunned silence followed on the other end of the line. Blake ended the call, slipping the phone back into his pocket. He glanced down at Buster, who was watching him with trusting eyes.

"Come on, buddy," Blake said, patting Buster's head. "We've got more ridiculous adventures ahead."

Together, they walked into the night, ready for whatever absurdity came next. They took a taxi and ventured their way out from the cold city as they got home.

Oh. Now it's time for your narration. Narrate your head off.

"See, as a kid, I've faced all the problems I had. And most of the time, I was the troublemaker. Wasn't I, Buster? And I miss the old taxi driver we had when we came here. This guy never speaks!" Blake rambled on, oblivious to the growing irritation of the driver.

Buster curled his tail and made himself comfortable, sensing it was going to be a long ride home.

"See, I broke..." Blake started, as—

"Can you just pipe down, you filthy knob head!" the taxi driver moaned, visibly frustrated.

"Well, now. There's quite no need to be rude. Don't blame me, I talk my head off!" Blake said, trying to convince him to shut hell up.

The taxi then immediately stopped with sudden haste in the middle of nowhere, near some tall sets of dark, green grass that stood unusually tall. The place was dark, dark. DARK! And it was a windy, cold, and eerie night.

"Why'd you stop the taxi for, Mr. Pipin'?" Blake snapped, feeling insecure.

The taxi driver pivoted with deliberate slowness, his eyes glinting with a blend of irritation and a more sinister undertone. "You prattle incessantly, child. And now, you shall face the consequences."

Blake's heart pounded. Buster, attuned to the tension, emitted a low growl. The driver exited the taxi, leaving the door ajar. Blake observed as he vanished into the tall, shadowy grass.

"Remain here, Buster," Blake murmured, cautiously opening the door. He stepped into the ominous night, the wind howling around him. The grass rustled, and Blake discerned the driver's footsteps crunching on the gravel.

"Mr. Pipin'!" Blake called out, striving to keep his voice steady. "What's transpiring? You imbecile, it's the dead of night and you're merely floundering about!"

No response. Blake inhaled deeply and pursued the sound of the footsteps. The darkness seemed to envelop him, and he could scarcely see a few feet ahead. Abruptly, he stumbled upon a small clearing. There, in the center, stood the driver, accompanied by several ruffians, all glaring menacingly at Blake.

"Now, heed my words!" the taxi driver, or Pipin' as Blake referred to him, bellowed. "Observe these individuals! They will ensure you bleed until you apologize for labeling me a 'halfwit'! You have no comprehension of my true identity!" His voice dripped with malice as the crooks huffed and scowled, their scarred visages menacing.

Blake's eyes widened as he realized the gravity of the situation. "What's your true identity, Spiderman? You need to chill, man."

The driver's eyes narrowed. "You think this is a joke? You've been running your mouth since you got in my cab. Now, you'll pay the price."

As you might have surmised, Blake remained utterly unperturbed!

"Can we dispense with all this perilous violence? I'm not particularly fond of it! I've already witnessed ample bloodshed! Or do you wish to persist?" Blake called out. I suppose they'll have to...

"Silence and engage in combat!" one of the voices demanded!

One of them came running towards Blake, and—bam!— In a flash, Blake stabbed him in the back! Then, he jabbed, then he backed his leg and actually pulled the guy's leg and smashed it on the other guy's face! And then, in a flash, he took his knife and stabbed him in the neck! And then, in a truly spectacular display of strength and agility, he smashed both of their heads together, breaking their bones!

But that wasn't all. As another came running, he was ready for them. He grabbed Blake and strangled him! Then, in a flash, Blake clenched his fists and knocked on his face with his elbows! And as the crook's nose bled heavily.

The guy with the "1000" muscles grabbed Blake's head with the help of two others! And then, another one! In a thrilling turn of events, all four of them, except for the one who died, formed a circle around Blake and began strangling him! Blake is searching for his breath when Buster made an entry to the scene, biting the man with bleeding nose.

Blake grabbed the opportunity to kick the man with a bleeding nose in the face, making a hole in the circle! Then, he pulled his knife, stabbed it into the man's hand, punched him to the ground, and watched as blood gushed onto the dark path. The muscular man was the last to remain and he took Blake's knife and came to stab him in the face and on that split second, Blake's instincts kicked in and he ducked just in time, narrowly avoiding the blade. "Nice try, muscle man, but you're not the first to underestimate me."

With a swift move, Blake grabbed the thug's wrist, twisting it until the knife clattered to the ground. "You know, you really should have stayed in the gym. This isn't your scene."

Blake delivered a powerful punch to the thug's jaw, sending him reeling backward. The thug stumbled, trying to regain his balance, but Blake was relentless. He followed up with a series of rapid punches, each one landing with precision.

The thug's eyes widened in shock as he realized he was outmatched. "You... you can't do this," he stammered.

Blake smirked. "Oh, I can, and I will." With one final, devastating blow, Blake knocked the thug out cold. He stood over the unconscious body, catching his breath.

What happened to Mr. Pipin? Well, he made a run for his life a long time ago!

"Well, that was a workout," Blake muttered, wiping the sweat from his brow. He glanced around, making sure there were no more surprises. "Buster, let's get out of here."

Buster trotted over, his tail wagging. Blake knelt down and ruffled the dog's fur. "Good job, buddy. We make a pretty good team, don't we?"

Blake stood up, dusted himself off, and looked around. 'Well, that was a fun little scuffle,' he said, grinning. 'But seriously, folks, if I wanted to be strangled by a bunch of goons, I would have just gone to my family reunion!'

He turned to Buster, who was wagging his tail enthusiastically. 'Buster, my loyal sidekick, you saved the day again! If only you could also save me from my terrible jokes.'

Blake stretched and yawned. 'Alright, let's get out of here before Pipin' decides to come back with more of his goon squad. I swear, that guy has more issues than a magazine subscription!'

With that, Blake and Buster walked away from the scene, ready for whatever the next chapter had in store for them.

As they made their way back to the taxi, Blake couldn't help but chuckle. "You know, Buster, I think we just found our new cardio routine. Who needs a gym membership when you've got thugs to take down?"

They climbed into the taxi, and Blake took the wheel. "Alright, let's get home. We've had enough excitement for one night."

As they drove off into the night, Blake glanced at Buster. "You know, buddy, I think we're going to be just fine. No matter what comes our way, we'll face it together."

And with that, they disappeared into the darkness, ready for whatever adventures awaited them next.

Let's go to the next chapter, shall we? Yep. Okay!

II
MURDER OF A TEEN

The night was still young, but Blake's mind was already reeling from the unexpected encounter with Mr. Pipin' and his goons. As they drive through the dark, eerie streets, Blake couldn't shake the feeling that something was amiss.

"Alright, buddy," Blake muttered, glancing down at Buster. "Let's head back and figure out our next move. There's something strange going on, and I don't like it one bit."

They made their way through the city, the distant sounds of sirens and the occasional car engine echoing in the background. The familiar scent of damp earth and faint smoke filled the air, a constant reminder of the city's restless nature.

As they approached Blake's apartment, a sense of unease settled over him. The door was slightly ajar, a faint light flickering from within. Blake's hand instinctively moved to his weapon, and Buster's ears perked up, sensing the tension.

"Stay close," Blake whispered to Buster, pushing the door open with a cautious hand.

The apartment was eerily quiet, the shadows cast by the flickering light creating an unsettling atmosphere. Blake moved silently, his eyes scanning every corner for any sign of an intruder. Buster followed closely, his nose twitching as he picked up unfamiliar scents.

As they entered the living room, Blake's eyes fell on a figure slumped on the couch. His heart skipped a beat as he recognized the face – a young girl, barely in her teens, with a lifeless expression.

"What the hell..." Blake muttered, rushing to the girl's side. He checked for a pulse, but there was none. She was gone.

Buster whimpered softly, sensing the gravity of the situation. Blake's mind raced as he tried to piece together what had happened.

His eyes suddenly focused on a small piece of paper with a handwritten note under her arms that read, "A gift from Mr. Phantom's household to my loyal servant."

Blake knew he had to report this to the authorities. He quickly dialed the police, explaining the situation and requesting immediate assistance. Within minutes, the apartment was swarming with officers, their radios crackling with urgent chatter.

"Sir, we need you to step outside," one of the officers instructed Blake. "We'll handle this from here."

Blake nodded, his mind still racing. He and Buster waited outside, the cold night air doing little to calm his nerves. After what felt like eternity, a detective approached him.

"Mr. Hunter. I'm Detective Ramirez," the detective introduced himself. "We need to ask you a few questions about the girl inside."

Blake's mind raced. How on earth does a detective know the name of the most idiotic mercenary? He thought, but his expression remained unreadable, betraying no hint of the confusion brewing within him.

Blake recounted everything he knew, from finding the girl to the message left by The Phantom. Detective Ramirez listened intently, taking notes, and nodding occasionally.

"We'll need to contact the girl's family," Ramirez said. "Do you have any idea who she might be?"

Blake shook his head. "No, but I have a feeling this isn't a random act. There's something more to this."

The detective nodded. "We'll look into it. In the meantime, I suggest you stay vigilant. If the Phantom's followers are involved, this could get dangerous."

Blake and Buster returned to their warehouse (which was basically a deserted place full of barrels), the weight of the situation was heavy on their shoulders. The next morning, Blake received a call from Detective Ramirez.

"Mr. Hunter, we've identified the girl," Ramirez said. "Her name was Emily. She was an activist, known for protesting against mercenaries and their activities. It seems she made some powerful enemies."

Blake almost asked Emily's first name but instead questioned, "So, was she targeted for her activism?"

"That's what it looks like," Ramirez confirmed. "We're still investigating, but it's clear she was a threat to someone. And they wanted to send a message."

Blake's resolve hardened. "Thank you, Detective. I'll be in touch if I find anything."

As he hung up the phone, Blake turned to Buster. "Alright, buddy. We've got a new mission. We're going to find out who did this to Emily and make sure they pay." Buster had a moment to acknowledge the fact that Blake cared about this. He looked at Blake, bewildered in his sight.

"I know, bud. It's weird." Blake sighed, as Buster was totally baffled.

Blake roared with laughter. "Oh, Buster, did you really think I'd turn in such a stellar performance with the detective because I care about some random girl's death? The fact that she 'hates mercenaries' just makes me chuckle.

If what I see and suspect is leading me in the right direction, then Ramirez is the killer. It is his perfect plan, but poor execution.

Oh, yeah! How do I know this? That's simple. Ramirez had a literal knife under his pocket and that girl was bleeding like she'd been stabbed! How do I know I'm not hallucinating?" Blake brandished the bloody knife he'd snatched when the detective wasn't looking.

Blake continued, "I also have other reasons to believe, since Ramirez could find the girl's name so quickly, but pretends he doesn't know Phantom is dead! Buster, my senses tell me the officer is trying to cover something up. I know this rogue detective joined Phantom's gang a long time ago! All of Phantom's people know that I'm their enemy now! He should have used his weapon, numbskull"

"Soon, that knucklehead will come here to take us down and reclaim the knife" "That's why I packed all the weapons, wait! I forgot. It's okay!" Blake yawned. "You ready, Buster? It's one gang against one genius, it's me!". Buster barked in agreement, ready for the upcoming challenge.

Blake sneered as a gunshot rang in the distance.

Blake gathered his gear, laser focused on the task at hand - smashing heads and grabbing cash!

The night was foggy and ghostly, or should I say ghastly? Well, it looked like nobody had shown up. He probably wasn't foolish enough to bring a bunch of people to kill a dog and a genius, right? Hmm... think again. Turns out you're smart and dead wrong. They were approaching from the left, and... maybe I should zip it now.

"Wait! Buster, a quick update, bud! 20... 21... 22 um... 26 people against one dog and a genius! Surely, they can't handle that! Can they? Oh gosh, we're doomed, Buster!" Blake exclaimed, turning to see an empty spot where Buster had been sitting. "BUSTER? BUDDY? NO!"

"Hands up! Or else we'll blast your ugly face, idiot! Tell me where our boss is?" Ramirez yelled on the top of his lungs.

Blake almost peed his pants. Yeah, sure! He could deal with a few 15-17 people, with knives. But machine guns! Those MG-42s made him feel they were German. But he gathered courage and managed to put up a bold front.

"No offense, bub! But your face is uglier!" Blake said, as they pointed the guns at him scowling at him! "Wait! Wait! Who's your boss? Lloyd Fredendall?" Blake said as they started firing! He quickly kicked the barrels and jumped into one of them, only to see Buster was inside it, shut the lid, as many of those blue barrels, which were stacked up, started to roll and this was starting to look like a game of crazy dominos, as both of them went rolling down in insane speeds!

"Buster! Nobody can separate us! Nobody!" Blake said as he hugged Buster (who was almost suffocated in this dark, enclosed, tiny place! But did those barrels manage to roll on them? Well, apparently half of those barrels were empty, like I told you, but the remaining half was filled with acetone, and Blake had a plan.

Those barrels came rolling down, as bullets were fired at the barrels, or in the speed the barrels were coming in, they would get trampled! And when they shot at acetone barrels... Um... Can we not talk about this? It's extremely violent and I'll get sued. Yep. Burned. Alive. Gore.

But what happened to the protagonists? They were definitely alive! The barrels (empty ones, of course!) protected them from the fire! And the fact that they were inside one of those barrels, didn't mean they were completely unharmed! Blake's arm tore, with blood leaking, as if it were a blood bag, when they rolled down.

Blake and Buster found themselves nestled inside the empty barrel, rolling at an incredible speed. The adrenaline rush was undeniable, but so was the danger around them. They could hear the bullets ricocheting off the barrels and the deafening sound of explosions as the acetone barrels ignited. It felt like a chaotic symphony of destruction.

However, Blake's quick thinking paid off. The empty barrel they were in acted as a protective shell, shielding them from the worst of the chaos. When the tumbling finally stopped, Blake carefully opened the lid, peeking out to assess the situation.

The warehouse was in disarray, with flames dancing around and the smell of smoke thick in the air. Despite the destruction, Blake and Buster were unharmed to a certain extent.

Now, they needed a plan to escape the warehouse and evade their pursuers. Using the confusion and chaos to their advantage, they crept through the shadows, avoiding the remaining adversaries and making their way to safety.

Blake, ever resourceful, quickly scanned the area for an exit. They needed to leave the warehouse and find a safe place to regroup and plan their next steps. As they moved cautiously through the wreckage, they stumbled upon a hidden passageway, partially obscured by fallen crates.

Blake and Buster had barely escaped the chaos of the warehouse. As they stumbled through the darkened streets, Blake felt a sharp pain in his arm. He glanced down and saw blood pouring from a deep gash. The adrenaline was wearing off, and the reality of his injury was setting in.

"Dammit," Blake muttered, gritting his teeth. "This isn't good."

Buster whimpered, sensing his partner's distress. They needed to find a safe place to tend to the wound. Blake spotted an alleyway and ducked into it.

"Alright, buddy," Blake said, his voice strained. "We need to stop this bleeding."

He pulled out a small towel from his coat and pressed it firmly against the wound, wincing as the pain shot through his arm. "Apply pressure," he reminded himself, trying to stay focused. "Keep it elevated."

Blake raised his injured arm above heart level, using his other hand to hold the cloth in place. The bleeding slowed, but it wasn't enough. He needed to clean the wound and bandage it properly.

"Stay with me, Buster," Blake said, his vision starting to blur. "I need you to keep watch."

Buster barked softly, his eyes scanning the alley for any signs of danger. Blake tells himself not to give up at this moment and waiting for the blood to stop. He know it is not safe to stay here for long, so he started to walk towards his nearby hideout with caution.

With Buster by his side, Blake pushed through the passage once he recovered, hoping it would lead them to freedom. The passage was narrow and dark, but determination and adrenaline kept them going. Eventually, they emerged into the cool night air, far from chaos behind them.

Their journey was far from over, but for now, they had managed to survive another dangerous encounter. Blake and Buster looked at each other, knowing that their bond and quick thinking had carried them through once again.

Blake and Buster moved stealthily through the darkened streets, their senses heightened and their resolve unshakable. The city was alive with danger, and they knew they had to remain vigilant. The warehouse encounter had shaken them, but Blake's cunning had kept them alive.

As they made their way to a safehouse, Blake took a deep breath and reached for the antiseptic wipes in the first aid kit. He carefully cleaned the wound, gritting his teeth against the pain.

"Almost there," Blake muttered, his hands shaking. He grabbed a roll of sterile bandages and began wrapping them around his arm, making sure the wound was covered and secure. "Snug, but not too tight," he reminded himself.

As he finished bandaging the wound, Blake felt a wave of dizziness wash over him. He knew he needed to stay hydrated and warm to prevent shock. He reached for a bottle of water and took a few sips, then pulled out a blanket and wrapped it around himself.

"Hang in there, Blake," he whispered, trying to stay conscious. "You've been through worse."

Buster nudged his leg, offering comfort and support. Blake smiled weakly, grateful for his loyal companion. "Thanks, buddy. I couldn't do this without you."

Blake knew he needed to find help soon, but for now, he had done everything he could to stabilize his condition. He leaned back against the wall, taking deep breaths and trying to stay alert.

Blake knew he couldn't stay in the alley any longer. With Buster by his side, he mustered the strength to stand up and began making his way to the safehouse. The journey through the darkened streets was fraught with danger, but Blake's resolve remained unshakable.

"Come on, Buster," Blake whispered, as they approached the entrance to the hidden apartment. He pressed a series of buttons on a concealed panel, and the door slid open. They quickly stepped inside, and Blake activated the security system, ensuring they were safe for the time being.

Blake's safehouse was a small, hidden apartment in the heart of the city, stocked with weapons, supplies, and a secure communication setup. It was here that he and Buster could regroup and plan their next move. As they entered the apartment, Blake activated the security system and began to review the events of the past few days.

Blake somehow managed to stood up, trying to shake off the unbearable pain but he just couldn't, as he sat down, his life almost over, as his third act flashbacks flashed beneath his eyes.

Blake's life was once filled with happiness and purpose. In his mid-20s, he had a stable job as a bank accountant. He enjoyed his work and found fulfillment in the simple routines of daily life. His closest companion was his loyal dog, Buster, who had been with him since he was a teenager. Blake had a small circle of friends and a content existence.

The day began like any other, with the hum of activity filling the bank. Blake sat at his desk, immersed in paperwork, the steady rhythm of his pen scratching against paper grounding him in the mundane. But then, a familiar burst of voices broke through the monotony.

"Hey, Mom! Dad! Jake!" Blake called out, his face lighting up as he spotted his family approaching. He waved them over, his heart swelling with unexpected joy.

His mother's eyes sparkled with warmth as she spoke. "We thought we'd surprise you. Jake's been begging to see where his big brother works."

Jake, a bright-eyed ten-year-old, darted forward, his excitement bubbling over. "This place is so cool, Blake! Can I sit at your desk?"

Blake chuckled, ruffling Jake's hair. "Of course, buddy. Just don't mess up my papers, alright? I've got a system here."

As Jake climbed into the chair, Blake's father placed a firm, reassuring hand on his shoulder. "We're proud of you, son. You've come a long way."

Blake felt a surge of pride and gratitude. "Thanks, Dad. That means a lot." For a moment, the world felt perfect—simple, even.

But then the phone rang, shattering the tranquility. Blake's expression shifted as he answered, his tone growing tense. The conversation escalated quickly, his voice sharp with frustration. Finally, after a long pause, he said with firm hesitation, "No, I can't do that."

As he hung up, his father's brow furrowed with concern. "Everything alright, Blake?"

Blake forced a smile, brushing off the question. "It's routine, Dad. Nothing to worry about."

He turned his attention toward his manager's office, where two men were leaving in a flurry of heated words. Their backs were to him, but the tension in their movements was palpable. Blake's manager emerged moments later, his face lined with worry.

"You were right about what you said," the manager admitted, his voice low. "But I'm afraid of the consequences. Please, Blake, make sure the paperwork is flawless—no gaps, no room for error."

Blake nodded, his confidence unwavering. "I've got it covered. Every detail is accounted for."

The manager hesitated, then sighed. "Alright. I'm stepping out for lunch. Let me know if anything urgent comes up." With that, he left, the door swinging shut behind him.

Blake turned back to his family, ready to pick up where they'd left off. But before he could speak, the world erupted.

A deafening explosion tore through the building, the force of it throwing Jake from the chair. Blake was hurled backward, his head slamming against the desk. The air filled with smoke, debris, and the piercing wail of alarms. The acrid scent of burning materials stung his nostrils as chaos consumed the room.

Blake's ears rang as he struggled to his feet, his vision swimming. "Mom! Dad! Jake!" he shouted, his voice raw with panic. He stumbled through the wreckage, his heart pounding as he searched desperately for his family.

Through the haze, he spotted his mother's scarf, torn and bloodied, lying amidst the rubble. His chest tightened as he pushed forward, calling out their names. "Mom! Dad! Jake!" Each cry was met with silence, the weight of dread pressing down on him.

He found Jake first, crumpled on the ground, his small frame battered but breathing. Blake dropped to his knees, his hands trembling as he checked for injuries. "Jake, buddy, stay with me," he whispered, his voice breaking. "I've got you."

Jake's eyes fluttered open, filled with pain and confusion. "Blake... what happened?"

Blake swallowed hard, forcing himself to stay calm. "It's going to be okay, Jake. I promise."

But as he looked around, the devastation became clearer. His parents were nowhere to be seen, and the realization hit him like a blow to the chest. The weight of loss and guilt threatened to consume him, but he pushed it aside, focusing on Jake.

"I'll get you out of here," Blake said, his voice steady despite the storm raging inside him. He lifted Jake into his arms, shielding him from the falling debris as he made his way toward the exit.

The world outside was a blur of sirens and shouting, but Blake's focus remained on his brother. As he handed Jake over to the paramedics, he turned back toward the wreckage, his heart heavy with the knowledge that his life would never be the same.

As they made their way through the wreckage, Blake's vision began to fade. He could hear Buster barking frantically in the distance, but the pain and exhaustion were overwhelming.

"Hang on, Jake," Blake whispered, his voice growing weaker. "We're almost there."

But before they could reach safety, Blake collapsed, his strength finally giving out. The last thing he heard was Buster's desperate barking, and then everything went black.

Blake's physical wounds healed, but the emotional scars ran deep. He was left with nothing—no family, no home, no job. The trauma of the attack and the loss of his parents left him broken and bankrupt. Desperate and with nowhere else to turn, Blake found himself drawn into the criminal underworld.

He joined a gang led by a man named Jonathan, who promised him a way to rebuild his life. The gang worked for powerful corporations, taking on dangerous missions to eliminate bad gangsters and rivals. The money was good, and for a while, Blake felt a sense of purpose again. He became skilled in combat and strategy, earning the respect of his fellow gang members.

Blake had been working with Jonathan's gang for a few months now, taking on dangerous missions and earning good money. His reputation within the gang was growing very soon. But Blake's primary concern was always his little brother, Jake, who had survived the bomb attack with him.

Jake had been staying with Blake, trying to rebuild their lives together. Blake did everything he could to protect Jake from the dangers of the criminal world, but it was becoming increasingly difficult. Jake was curious and eager to help, and Blake couldn't always keep him out of harm's way.

One evening, Blake returned to their hideout after a successful mission. He found Jake sitting on the couch, looking anxious.

"Hey, Jake," Blake said, ruffling his brother's hair. "What's wrong?"

Jake looked up, his eyes filled with worry. "Blake, I... I did something bad."

Blake's heart sank. "What do you mean, Jake? What happened?"

Jake hesitated, then took a deep breath. "I wanted to help you, so I followed you on your mission. I saw you take down that guy, and I thought I could do it too. But... but I messed up. I killed someone, Blake. I didn't mean to, but I did."

Blake's blood ran cold. "Jake, you shouldn't have been there. You know how dangerous it is."

"I know," Jake said, tears streaming down his face. "I'm sorry, Blake. I just wanted to help."

Blake pulled Jake into a tight embrace. "It's okay, Jake. We'll figure this out. Just stay with me, alright?"

But before Blake could say anything more, the door to the hideout burst open. Jonathan and his men stormed in, their faces twisted with anger.

"Blake, we need to talk," Jonathan said, his voice cold and menacing.

Blake stood protectively in front of Jake. "What's going on, Jonathan?"

Jonathan's eyes narrowed. "Your little brother here killed one of our clients. That's a problem, Blake. A big problem."

Blake's heart pounded in his chest. "It was an accident, Jonathan. He's just a kid. We'll make it right."

Jonathan shook his head. "No, Blake. This is beyond fixing. We have rules, and those rules need to be enforced."

Before Blake could react, Jonathan pulled out a gun and aimed it at Jake. "I'm sorry, Blake. But this is how it has to be."

"NO!" Blake screamed, lunging forward to shield Jake. But it was too late. The gunshot echoed through the room, and Jake's body went limp in Blake's arms.

"Jake! No, no, no!" Blake cried, tears streaming down his face. He cradled his brother's lifeless body, his heart breaking into a million pieces.

Jonathan holstered his gun, his expression cold and unfeeling. "This is the price of failure, Blake. Remember that."

Blake's grief quickly turned to rage. He gently laid Jake's body down and stood up, his eyes blazing with fury. "You ungrateful monster!... you killed him. I'll kill you for this."

Jonathan smirked. "I'd like to see you try."

With a roar of anger, Blake charged at Jonathan, his fists flying. The room erupted into chaos as Blake fought with everything he had, driven by a burning desire for revenge. Jonathan's men tried to intervene, but Blake was unstoppable, his rage giving him strength. Lying on the ground, Jonathan was bleeding profusely.

Blake stood over Jonathan's motionless body, his chest heaving with exertion. He had avenged Jake, but the victory felt hollow. He had lost the only family he had left, and the pain was unbearable.

Blake collapsed to the floor; his body wracked with sobs. Buster, who had been hiding during the fight, came over and nuzzled Blake's hand, offering comfort.

"I'm sorry, Jake," Blake whispered, his voice choked with emotion as tears rolled down. "I couldn't protect you. But I promise, I'll make them all pay."

From that moment on, Blake vowed to trust no one and to do whatever it took to survive. He became a cold and calculating mercenary, willing to kill anyone who dared to cross him. Good people, bad people—it didn't matter. Blake's only concern was protecting himself and Buster.

The pursuit of money and power became his driving force. Each mission, each kill, brought him closer to financial security and a sense of control over his life. But the cost was high. Blake's humanity eroded with each act of violence, and he became a shadow of the man he once was.

Years of navigating the treacherous world of mercenaries had taken their toll on Blake. He became cynical and detached, prioritizing survival and profit over the ideals that once drove him. The pursuit of money and power had led him down a dark path, but deep down, the desire to make amends and find redemption still lingered.

But now, he wanted to get out of all this. For him, all that he wanted was a good life for him and Buster. Part of him didn't want to kill anyone, but he had to. Once he started, he couldn't stop, that's the art of hell and heaven. Either you need to have a pure, angelic soul to reach heaven or a totally evil life with many crimes against you that would bring you to hell. But if you are walking on the middle, you belong to nowhere and almost every single common person life ends up here.

Most people who went from good to bad did so because of tragedies that changed their lives, but no one can change their life once they've gone bad, they're just supposed to live as bad. But our protagonist is someone who is anything but ordinary!

Remember when I said what happens if Blake gets hired by both sides of the ethical spectrum at the same time? And which side should he choose?

I know you're thinking, Blake's at a crossroads, and the stakes couldn't be higher. The Phantom sounds like a mysterious and formidable group. Will they be the ones to influence Blake's decision, or will he find a way to navigate the murky waters of ethical dilemmas on his own?

Here's a thought: What if Blake's decision isn't just about choosing sides, but about redefining the rules of the game altogether? Maybe he can find a third way that neither side is expecting. What do you think? Finish both sides... And to do that, he had to be smart! Really smart!

III

THE AMBUSH
AND A
CLIFFHANGER

Suddenly Blake received a message "Surrender; Our deal is over" in Blake's phone and Buster sense something bad. Goodman's ten henchmen were scattered throughout the house, ready for a fight. Blake grabbed a frying pan from the kitchen, swinging it like a pro chef in a cooking show gone wrong. The first thug went down with a loud clang, more surprised than hurt.

"Well, both deal and life is over! I guess!" Blake said as he dodged a knife throw straight to his head. "Whoo! That was close!" he sighed.

Blake turned to the surveillance security camera, "Seriously, who knew a frying pan could be this effective?" Buster, ever the loyal companion, lunged at another henchman, using his powerful jaws to disarm him. The thug's scream was more of a high-pitched yelp, like a cartoon character stepping on a rake. Blake moved through the house with agility, using whatever he could find as a weapon. A rolling pin became a makeshift club, and he wielded it like a baker on a mission. "Time to roll out the dough!" he quipped, knocking out another thug.

A toaster was hurled with deadly accuracy, hitting a henchman square in the face. "Toast's ready!" Blake shouted, barely containing his laughter. He grabbed a kitchen knife and wielded it with expert skill, slicing through the air with precision. "Physics? who needs it?" he joked, as the knife seemed to defy gravity.

Buster was right there with him, taking down enemies with a ferocity that matched Blake's own. One thug tried to hide behind a refrigerator, but Blake simply opened the door and slammed it shut on him. "Chill out, buddy," he said with a grin.

Despite the chaos, Blake's right arm took a heavy hit, but he fought through the pain. He and Buster were a well-oiled machine, working in tandem to take down the henchmen one by one. The house was filled with the sounds of clashing metal, breaking glass, and the grunts of combat.

At one point, Blake paused to catch his breath and looked directly at the surveillance security camera. "You ever wonder why bad guys always attack one at a time? Makes my job a lot easier." He winked before diving back into the fray.

Finally, as the last of the Goodman's men lay defeated, Blake sent a final message from his phone: "I would surrender but after all your guys are dead!" The words were a stark reminder of the cost of crossing Blake and his loyal companion, but with a touch of dark humor that only Blake could pull off.

The Phantom's men gathered in a dimly lit room, the air thick with tension. The once-mighty leader, Phantom, had been dead for six days, and Blake had taken down 30-40 of their members. The Goodman's forces were also dwindling, thanks to Blake's relentless assault. It was clear that something had to change.

"Blake is a menace," one of the Phantom's lieutenants growled, slamming his fist on the table. "We can't keep losing men like this. Every day, we grow weaker while he grows bolder."

"We need a new strategy," another chimed in, his voice laced with frustration. "We can't fight him alone. We need to join forces with the Goodman."

The room fell silent as the weight of the suggestion sank in. The Phantom's men had always prided themselves on their independence, their ability to handle any threat on their own. But desperate times called for desperate measures.

"Are we really considering this?" a third lieutenant asked, his voice tinged with disbelief. "The Goodman is our enemy. We've fought against him for years."

"Blake is a bigger threat," the first lieutenant replied, his tone resolute. "If we don't stop him, there won't be any of us left to fight the Goodman. We have to put our differences aside, at least for now."

Reluctantly, the Phantom's men agreed to reach out to the Goodman. A meeting was arranged in a neutral location, a rundown warehouse on the outskirts of the city. The tension was palpable as they prepared for the encounter, each man acutely aware of the stakes.

The warehouse was eerily quiet as the Phantom's men and the Goodman's forces faced each other. The air was thick with mistrust, but both sides knew they had no choice but to cooperate.

"We need to take down Blake," the Goodman said, breaking the silence. His voice was cold and calculating. "He's been a thorn in both our sides for too long. If we don't act now, he'll destroy us all."

The Phantom's men nodded in agreement. "We propose an alliance," their leader said, stepping forward. "Together, we can outnumber and outsmart him. We have the resources, and you have the manpower. It's the only way."

Goodman considered the offer for a moment before nodding. "Agreed. But we need a plan. Blake is cunning and resourceful. He won't fall for just any trap."

The two groups spent hours strategizing, mapping out Blake's known hideouts and routines. They decided to lure him into a trap, using false information to draw him into a secluded location where they could ambush him.

"We'll need to be careful," Goodman warned. "Blake is always one step ahead. We can't afford to make any mistakes."

"We'll make it convincing," the Phantom's leader assured him. "We'll use one of our own as bait. Someone he trusts."

"But Blake trusts no one," a lieutenant pointed out. "How do we get him to take the bait?"

"We don't need him to trust anyone," the Goodman replied with a sly smile. "We just need to make him think he's found a weakness. We'll plant false information in a way that makes it look like a slip-up. Blake won't be able to resist investigating."

The plan was set, and the alliance was forged. As they left the warehouse, both sides knew that this was their last chance to take down Blake. Failure was not an option.

The Phantom's men selected one of their most trusted members to act as the bait. He was given a false story to feed to Blake, claiming to have information about Goodman's whereabouts. The bait was set, and the trap was ready.

Blake, always on the lookout for an opportunity to strike, took the bait. He and Buster set off for the location, unaware of the trap that awaited them. As they approached the secluded location, Blake's senses were on high alert. The place seemed deserted, but Blake knew better than to let his guard down.

As Blake and Buster moved deeper into the area, the ambush was sprung. The forces of Phantom and Goodman emerged from the shadows surrounding Blake and Buster. The air was thick with tension, and the odds seemed insurmountable.

"Looks like we've got you now," the Goodman sneered, stepping forward with a smug grin.

Blake smirked, his eyes glinting with defiance. "You think this is the end? You have no idea what you're up against."

With a dramatic snap of his fingers, Blake shouted, "Money! Money! Money!" To everyone's astonishment, half of the Goodman's men suddenly turned on their comrades, their eyes gleaming with greed.

"Sorry, boss," one of the turncoats said, shrugging. "But Blake's offering a better deal."

The Goodman's jaw dropped. "You traitors! How much did he pay you?"

Blake chuckled. "Let's just say, enough to buy loyalty."

The fight that ensued was nothing short of epic. Blake and Buster fought with everything they had, using their surroundings to their advantage. The Phantom's men and the Goodman's forces were relentless, but Blake's determination was unyielding.

Blake grabbed a nearby metal pipe, swinging it with brutal force. The first thug crumpled to the ground, his weapon clattering away. Buster, ever the loyal companion, lunged at another henchman, his powerful jaws clamping down on the man's arm. The thug screamed, trying to shake Buster off, but the dog held firm.

The warehouse echoed with the sounds of combat, the air thick with the scent of sweat and blood. Blake moved with a deadly grace, his movements were precise and efficient. He used the environment to his advantage, ducking behind crates and using them as shields. A well-aimed kick sent another thug sprawling into a stack of barrels, which toppled over with a deafening crash.

Despite being outnumbered, Blake and Buster managed to hold their own, taking down enemy after enemy. Blake's fists were a blur as he delivered a series of rapid punches to a thug's midsection, finishing with a devastating uppercut that sent the man flying. Buster, meanwhile, had taken down two more henchmen, his growls echoing through the warehouse.

Just when it seemed like Blake and Buster might be overwhelmed, reinforcements arrived. A group of Blake's allies, who had been tracking the Phantom's men, burst into the warehouse, evening the odds. They charged into the fray with a battle cry, their weapons flashing in the dim light.

The battle raged on, but with the arrival of Blake's allies, the tide began to turn. The Phantom's men and the Goodman's forces found themselves on the defensive, struggling to hold their ground. Blake's allies fought with a ferocity that matched his own, their attacks coordinated and relentless.

As the fight reached its climax, Blake found himself face-to-face with the Goodman. The two locked eyes, their mutual hatred palpable. The Goodman sneered, raising his weapon.

"This ends now," Blake growled, his voice low and dangerous.

The Goodman lunged, but Blake was ready. He sidestepped the attack and delivered a powerful punch to Goodman's ribs. The Goodman staggered, but quickly recovered, swinging his weapon in a wide arc. Blake ducked under the swing and countered with a swift kick to Goodman's knee, causing him to stumble.

The two men circled each other, their movements tense and calculated. Blake could feel the adrenaline coursing through his veins, his senses heightened. He knew this fight would determine the outcome of the battle.

With a roar, the Goodman charged again, but Blake met him head-on. The two clashed in a flurry of punches and kicks, each trying to gain the upper hand. Blake's allies continued to fight around them, their shouts and the sounds of combat filling the air.

Finally, with a well-placed strike, Blake disarmed the Goodman, sending his weapon skittering across the floor. The Goodman fell to his knees, gasping for breath. Blake stood over him, his expression cold and unyielding.

"It's over," Blake said, his voice steady. "You lose."

The Goodman looked up at Blake, his eyes filled with a mix of rage and defeat. "This isn't the end," he spat. "There will always be someone else."

Blake shook his head. "Not if I have anything to say about it."

As the warehouse fell silent, Blake's allies gathered around him, their expressions a mix of relief and exhaustion. The battle was won, but the war was far from over.

"This ends now," Blake growled, raising his weapon.

The Goodman smirked, his eyes glinting with malice. "Oh, I don't think so. You see, Blake, there's something you don't know."

Before Blake could react, the Goodman pressed a button on a remote control, and the warehouse was suddenly filled with the sound of ticking.

Blake's eyes widened in realization. "You rigged the place to blow."

Goodman's smirk widened. "Exactly. And now, we all go down together."

The ticking grew louder, and Blake knew they had only moments to escape. He turned to his allies, shouting for them to get out.

As the warehouse began to collapse around them, Blake and Buster fought their way through the chaos, determined to survive.

The warehouse was a scene of utter chaos. The ticking of the bombs grew louder, echoing through the cavernous space like a countdown to doom. Blake's heart pounded in his chest as he shouted for his allies to evacuate. "Everyone, move! Now!"

The Goodman's smirk never wavered as he watched the panic unfold. "You can't save them all, Blake," he taunted. "This place is going down, and so are you."

Blake ignored the taunts, his focus solely on getting his people to safety. He grabbed Buster by the collar and sprinted towards the nearest exit, dodging falling debris and the desperate attacks of the remaining henchmen. The ground beneath them shook violently, and the sound of explosions filled the air.

As Blake and Buster reached the exit, a massive explosion rocked the warehouse, sending a shockwave that knocked them off their feet. Blake hit the ground hard, his vision blurring as he struggled to stay conscious. He could hear the screams of his allies and the deafening roar of the collapsing building.

The Goodman, ever the opportunist, used the chaos to his advantage. He slipped through the shadows, avoiding the falling debris with practiced ease. His mind raced as he plotted his next move. Blake had been a formidable opponent, but Goodman was nothing if not resourceful.

As he made his way to a hidden exit, the Goodman couldn't help but chuckle to himself. "Blake may have won the battle, but the war is far from over," he muttered. He reached the exit and slipped out into the night, disappearing into the darkness.

The warehouse was reduced to a smoldering ruin, the once-mighty structure now a twisted heap of metal and concrete. The air was thick with smoke and dust, and the ground was littered with debris. Emergency responders arrived on the scene, their sirens wailing as they began the grim task of searching for survivors.

News of the explosion spread quickly, and soon the media was swarming the site, eager for any information. Reporters jostled for position, their cameras capturing the devastation. The headline on every news channel was the same: "Blake and Buster Presumed Dead in Warehouse Explosion."

Authorities launched an investigation into the explosion, determined to uncover the truth. They combed through the wreckage, searching for any clues that might explain what had happened. Forensic teams worked tirelessly, sifting through the debris and analyzing the evidence.

Despite their best efforts, they could find no trace of Blake or Buster. It was as if they had vanished into thin air. The lack of bodies only fueled the speculation and rumors. Some believed that Blake had somehow survived and was in hiding, while others were convinced that he had perished in the explosion.

The media frenzy surrounding Blake's presumed death showed no signs of abating. News outlets ran constant coverage, interviewing anyone who might have known Blake or had any information about the explosion. Conspiracy theories abounded, with some suggesting that Blake had faked his own death to escape his enemies.

Talk shows and news programs debated the mystery, with experts weighing in on the likelihood of Blake's survival. The public was captivated by the story, and Blake's name became a household word. His legend grew, and he was hailed as a hero by some and a villain by others. Yet, no one knew how Blake looked like.

Blake's allies were devastated by the loss. They gathered in secret, mourning the man who had led them with such courage and determination. They shared stories of his bravery and recounted the many battles they had fought together. Buster's absence was keenly felt, and they honored the loyal dog who had stood by Blake's side through thick and thin.

Despite their grief, Blake's allies knew that they had to carry on. They vowed to continue the fight in his name, determined to honor his legacy. They knew that the Goodman was still out there, and they were more resolved than ever to bring him to justice.

The Goodman wasted no time in capitalizing on Blake's presumed death. He moved quickly to consolidate his power, eliminating any rivals who might challenge his authority. He recruited new henchmen, bolstering his ranks and preparing for the next phase of his plan.

With Blake out of the picture, the Goodman felt invincible. He reveled in his newfound freedom, confident that no one could stand in his way. But deep down, he couldn't shake the nagging feeling that Blake might still be alive. The uncertainty gnawed at him, fueling his paranoia.

Blake's closest allies refused to accept his death without proof. They launched their own investigation, determined to uncover the truth. They scoured the city, following every lead and questioning anyone who might have information. Their search was relentless, driven by the hope that Blake and Buster might still be alive.

As they delved deeper into the mystery, they uncovered a web of deception and intrigue. They discovered that Goodman had orchestrated the explosion, and they began to piece together his plan. The more they learned, the more determined they became to find Blake and bring the Goodman to justice. Finally, there was no proof on whether to decide whether Blake was dead, so Blake was alive.

Even if Blake was alive, he was now the least of the gang's concerns. With no army left, he is like a wet kitten wandering in hurricane. He couldn't fight them back; he could barely fight off a sneeze at this point. How would he get back to his normal life? Well, I'd say this is the perfect moment to end in a cliffhanger.

IV
THE VIPERS

Blake and Buster, though separated from their allies, were very alive!

They had barely escaped the explosion, thanks to a hidden passageway that led them to an underground tunnel. The blast had injured them both, but their survival instincts had kicked in, keeping them moving forward.

The tunnel led to an abandoned subway station, a dark and desolate place where they could take a moment to regroup. Blake, his arm bandaged from the earlier injury, looked around for any signs of danger while Buster kept watch.

"We need to find a way out of this mess, Buster," Blake muttered, wincing from the pain in his arm. "We can't keep running forever."

As they navigated the subway tunnels, Blake's thoughts drifted to his allies. He hoped they were safe and that they would continue the fight. But for now, he had to focus on survival and finding a way to turn the tide.

Blake knew he couldn't take on Goodman's forces alone. He needed a plan, a way to gather new allies and resources.

His mind raced as he considered his options. There were still people in the city who owed him favors, and he intended to call them in.

The first step was to get out of the subway and find a safe place to regroup. Blake and Buster moved cautiously, staying in the shadows and avoiding detection. They emerged from the subway tunnels into a quiet alleyway, the cool night air a welcome relief from the stifling darkness of the tunnels.

Blake led Buster through the maze of backstreets, his senses on high alert. They needed to find a safehouse, a place where they could rest and plan their next move. As they moved through the city, Blake's thoughts turned to the future. He couldn't keep living like this, constantly on the run and fighting for survival. He wanted a better life for himself and Buster.

Finally, they reached an old, abandoned building that Blake had used as a hideout in the past. It wasn't much, but it would do for now. They slipped inside and secured the doors, making sure they were safe from any potential threats.

Blake collapsed onto a dusty old couch, exhaustion washing over him. Buster curled up beside him, resting his head on Blake's leg. Despite the chaos and danger, Blake felt a sense of determination. He knew that they could make it through this, as long as they stuck together.

"We'll figure this out, buddy," Blake said, stroking Buster's fur. "We're not done yet. Not by a long shot."

With renewed resolve, Blake began to formulate a plan. He would reach out to his old contacts, gather new allies, and find a way to take down Goodman once and for all. It wouldn't be easy, but Blake had faced impossible odds before, and he wasn't about to give up now.

As the first light of dawn began to filter through the broken windows, Blake knew that their journey was far from over. But for the first time in a long while, he felt a glimmer of hope. They had survived the explosion, and that meant they could survive whatever came next.

Blake and Buster were ready to face the challenges ahead, armed with their determination and the bond that had seen them through countless battles. The fight for justice and redemption was just beginning, and they were prepared to see it through to the end.

Blake and Buster spent the next few days recovering in the shadows of the abandoned building. The pain from Blake's injuries was a constant reminder of the danger they faced. Desperation gnawed at him, knowing that he couldn't fight this battle alone.

Blake reached out to his old contacts, hoping to find allies who could help him take down Goodman and The Phantom. But one by one, they turned him down. The responses were cold and unforgiving.

The phone buzzed sharply in the quiet room, cutting through Blake's scattered thoughts. He hesitated for a split second before picking up, already sensing the storm waiting on the other end.

"What now?" Blake said gruffly, trying to mask the fatigue creeping into his voice.

The response was immediate, sharp, and colder than he expected. "Blake, we've had enough. You've pushed us too far, and we're not risking our necks for you anymore."

Blake froze, the weight of the words hitting him like a fist to the gut. "What are you talking about?" he said, his voice tight with disbelief. "You know the stakes. You know why this fight matters!"

"Do we?" the voice snapped back, dripping with anger and frustration. "Because from where we stand, it looks like you've dragged us into chaos without a plan. Without an exit. You don't care about what it costs us, Blake. And we're done paying the price."

"You can't just walk away!" Blake barked, his grip tightening on the phone. "You think this is about me? It's bigger than all of us. If you don't stand with me now—"

"You're on your own," the voice interrupted, colder than ever. "We're not your safety net. Fight your war, Blake. But don't expect us to die for your mess."

The line went dead with a finality that made Blake feel like the ground had just shifted beneath him. He stared at the phone, the words echoing in his mind. For the first time, he truly felt the weight of his isolation. His chest tightened, but he forced himself to breathe, to steady his thoughts.

Left alone in the silence of the moment, Blake's jaw clenched as resolve burned in his gut. "Fine," he muttered to himself, his voice hard and low. "If I have to fight this alone, then so be it."

The rejections stung, deepening the sense of isolation that had settled over Blake like a dark cloud. It was clear that his past actions had burned too many bridges, and now he was paying the price.

As the rejections piled up, Blake's resolve began to waver. He was outnumbered and outgunned, with no one to turn to. The weight of his choices pressed down on him, and the once unbreakable determination started to crack.

Blake spent sleepless nights staring at the maps and intel spread out before him. He knew he couldn't win this fight through sheer force. He needed to outthink his enemies, to use their weaknesses against them.

Desperation gnawed at him, and the need for sustenance became a pressing concern. One evening, as hunger pangs grew unbearable, Blake decided to venture out into the city for food. He and Buster navigated the dark, narrow alleys, their senses on high alert for any signs of danger.

They arrived at a small, dingy hot dog stand tucked away in a forgotten corner of the city. The stand's flickering neon sign cast an eerie glow on the street. Blake approached the vendor, a grizzled old man with a weary expression.

"Two hot dogs," Blake said, his voice raspy from days of silence.

The vendor looked up, his tired eyes meeting Blake's. "Sorry, buddy, but there's only one left," he replied, lifting a hefty hot dog from the grill. "It's heavy."

Blake glanced down at Buster, who was standing by his side, looking up expectantly. "Make that two," Blake insisted. "One for me and one for my partner here."

The vendor chuckled, finally noticing Buster. "Alright, you got it," he said, splitting the hot dog and handing half to Blake and the other half to Buster.

As Blake took a bite, he felt a surge of energy. He glanced around, making sure no one was watching, and then leaned in closer to the vendor. "I need you to send a message for me."

The vendor raised an eyebrow. "To whom?"

Blake's eyes hardened. "To your boss" he said, showing the hot dog's package where "Goodman" was written. Bingo! "Tell him I'm not done yet. He can keep sending his goons, but I'll keep taking them down. One by one."

The vendor's expression shifted to one of concern. "You're playing a dangerous game, friend. I know my boss. He'll kill you in a second if he wanted!"

Blake smirked. "I know. But it's a game I intend to win and tell him to kill me!"

The vendor nodded, understanding the gravity of the message. "Consider it done. Stay safe out there."

Blake and Buster finished their meal and slipped back into the shadows, the weight of their situation pressing down on them. The message had been sent, and Blake knew it was only a matter of time before the Goodman responded.

As they navigated the dark streets, Blake's mind raced with thoughts of their next move. He couldn't rely on allies, but he could rely on his own skills and the bond he shared with Buster. They had to outthink and outmaneuver their enemies if they were to survive.

Blake knew that the path ahead would be fraught with danger, but he was determined to see it through. He and Buster would continue to fight, no matter the odds, until justice was served.

Blake and Buster spent the next few days recovering in the shadows, formulating a new plan. With no allies to rely on, Blake decided to infiltrate a local gang to survive and take down The Phantom's men. He set sights on a rough gang known as "The Vipers."

Blake knew he needed a unique approach to gain their trust. One evening, he approached The Vipers' hideout, a dingy bar filled with rough characters. With Buster by his side, Blake pushed open the door and stepped inside, immediately drawing the attention of the gang members.

A burly man with a scar running down his check approached Blake, eyeing him suspiciously. "Who the hell are you?"

Blake flashed a confident grin. "Name's Blake. Heard you guys could use some... entertainment."

The man raised an eyebrow. "Entertainment? This ain't no circus, pal."

Blake chuckled, pulling out a deck of cards from his pocket. "Maybe not, but I bet I can show you a trick or two." He started shuffling the cards with impressive speed and dexterity.

The gang members gathered around, intrigued by Blake's antics. The burly man crossed his arms, clearly unimpressed. "Alright, let's see what you've got."

Blake's grin widened. "Pick a card, any card." The man reluctantly drew a card from the deck, and Blake continued shuffling. "Now, watch closely."

With a flourish, Blake revealed the man's card, earning a few chuckles from the crowd. But he hasn't done yet. He threw the deck into the air, and in a blur of motion, he caught the exact card between his fingers. "Ta-da!"

The gang members erupted in laughter and applause. The burly man's stern expression softened slightly. "Not bad, not bad. But we ain't looking for a magician. Get the hell out of here before things get ugly."

Blake's smile faded, replaced by a steely determination. "Good, because I'm more than that. And I can make things uglier than you could ever possibly imagine, you—" He grinned, leaning in like he was sharing a secret. "—well, let's just say you're about to find out. Trust me, it's not gonna be pretty."

The men around him all pulled out their guns at once. Blake's eyes widened for a split second before a playful grin crept up. He gave a slow, dramatic look at the shiny pieces in their hands. "Ooh, look at this," Blake said, pointing at one of the guns. "Is this the latest model? I like the little shine—real classy. Does it come with a complimentary laser pointer, or is that extra?"

Tony, the leader, shot him a warning glare. "Put the guns down, guys. We don't need to shoot him. Yet."

Blake raised his hands mockingly in surrender, still smiling. "Whoa, Tony. I get it, you're the big boss here, but all this firepower's making me feel like I walked onto the set of an action movie. I should've worn my leather Jacket for this, it might have looked more convincing."

Tony sighed, rolling his eyes. "Just focus, Blake."

Blake straightened up and threw a casual glance at the men's weapons. "Well, alright. Welcome to the party. I hear you've got a problem with The Phantom's men. Let me help you out with that. I promise, I'm great at solving problems... *especially* when it involves big guns and with zero consequences."

The man standing next to Tony raised an eyebrow, eyeing Blake with suspicion. "And why should we trust you?"

Blake leaned in a little closer, still grinning. "Because I've got a score to settle with them," he said, tapping his chin thoughtfully. "And I've been practicing my aim in the mirror all week. Plus, I've never been *too* bad with a Nerf gun... so I figure, how hard could real ones be?"

After a long pause, the man reluctantly nodded. "Alright, Blake, we are in for just one time and nothing more. If you screw this up, you're out."

Blake shot him with a playful wink. "Don't worry, I've got perfect plan, but I will tell you when I'm not distracted by these shiny things, nodding at their guns."

One evening, as Blake and The Vipers prepped for their upcoming showdown with The Phantom's men, Blake casually leaned back and asked, "So, what's the deal with all this gang drama? I know it's common, but what's the real beef?"

Tony seemed to have his own zip code, shot Blake a look like he'd just smelled something foul. "The Phantom shot our leader—right in the groin. Can you believe that? Just walked up and popped him like it was no big deal!"

Blake's eyebrow arched, an almost smug smirk pulling at his lips. "Ouch. That's gotta hurt. I heard a guy named Blake killed The Phantom, though... Is that true?"

Tony froze mid-motion, his expression morphing into one of sheer disbelief. For a moment, it looked like he'd seen a ghost. "Wait, wait... what's your name again?" he stammered, the usual confidence in his voice slipping.

Blake leaned in with an infuriatingly cocky grin, his eyes glittering with mischief. "It's always Blake, Blake Hunter," he replied, his tone oozing nonchalance.

Tony's jaw nearly hit the floor. He stumbled back a step, pointing at Blake like he'd just uncovered some unfathomable secret. "You're kidding! Holy—You're the one who took down The Phantom?" The disbelief in his voice bordered on awe, mingled with a hint of fear.

Blake shrugged, casual as ever, his hands sliding into his pockets. "Guilty as charged," he said, cracking his knuckles. There was menace in his voice, but it was wrapped in a layer of laid-back confidence that made it all the more unnerving.

The man standing to Tony's right looked between the two of them, his face pale with shock. His gaze darted toward Tony, as though silently pleading for clarification, trying to make sense of the revelation. His fingers twitched nervously at his side.

Tony, shaking himself out of his stunned state, shot the man a sharp look and jerked his head toward the back. "Come with me," he said, his voice low and urgent.

They moved quickly down a narrow, dimly lit passage that led to the bar's back entrance, their footsteps echoing off the worn floorboards. Once they were alone, the air thickened with tension, a heated argument erupting between them. The man's voice rose and fell in sharp bursts, challenging Tony at every turn, but Tony's responses came back like a volley of sharp-edged daggers, each one cutting deeper into the man's defenses.

Finally, the argument reached a boiling point. There was a long pause, the kind of silence that hangs heavily in the air, ready to snap like a taut wire.

The man exhaled sharply, defeated but resolute. His lips twisted into a grimace as he muttered, "At your service, Tony... as always." His voice carried an edge of reluctant loyalty, a promise made through gritted teeth.

Tony smirked, a hint of satisfaction flickering in his eyes. He patted the man's shoulder with a casualness that belied the intensity of their conversation. "That's more like it."

Without another word, Tony turned back toward the main bar, leaving the man standing in the shadows, his shoulders squared but his jaw clenched in barely restrained frustration.

At the same time in other part of town, The Phantom's men gathered in the dimly lit room. The news that had just come in was a gut-punch. *Blake Hunter was alive.* The words rattled around the room like a ticking time bomb.

Aiden, the ripped leader, slammed his fist down on the table, making the other men jump as the wood groaned under the impact. His voice was like gravel when he spoke. "Blake Hunter is alive," he growled, his words low, but crackling with rage. "How the hell did this happen?"

The wiry man with a twitch in his eye was the first to speak up, his voice barely a squeak. "We got word from one of our informants. He saw Blake at a hot dog stand with his little dog."

Aiden's eyes narrowed, pupils burning with fury. "And you let him slip through your fingers?" His tone was colder than ice, and the room felt like it was shrinking in on itself. "You let Blake Hunter Walk free after all that? Do you have any idea what that means?"

The room fell dead silent. Every man there knew that this wasn't just another screw-up. This was big much bigger than they could even imagine.

Another man, tall, gangly, a guy who always seemed on edge, stepped forward, his voice tight with anxiety. "What do we do now, boss?"

Aiden stood still for a moment, taking a long breath to reign in the storm that was boiling inside him. His fingers twitched, ready to explode, but his face was a mask of cold calculation. "First, we make sure the Goodman doesn't get wind of this. If he finds out Blake's alive, we'll be buried before we even see it coming."

The men nodded, understanding the danger in their midst. It was clear now: *this* wasn't just about survival. This was about saving their necks from the hell storm that was Blake Hunter.

Aiden turned, pacing with a predatory calmness. "Second," he continued, find that hot dog vendor and make sure he never talks to anyone again, but let him live. You know what I mean, No one helps Blake Hunter. Not now, not ever."

The wiry man's eyes widened, and he swallowed hard, clearly nervous. "But boss... what if Blake comes after us? What if he finds out what we did?"

Aiden's gaze hardened. His jaw clenched so tightly it looked like it might crack. "If Blake comes after us..." He took a slow step forward, his voice dangerously calm. "Then we'll be ready. We don't just finish what we started—we *end* it. No more mistakes. This time, Blake doesn't get to walk away."

The air in the room felt heavy, suffocating. Every man in there could feel it, their backs against the wall, knowing there was no room for error. Blake Hunter wasn't just a ghost anymore. He was real, and he was coming.

The men scattered, each of them moving with a sense of grim determination. Failure wasn't an option. Not now. Not with Blake alive.

In the meantime, at Vipers' hideout, Blake and Buster were planning their next move, expecting the Phantom's men will come after the hot dog vendor. Confident but oblivious to the trap, The Phantom's men headed toward the location.

Blake, expecting The Phantom's move, rallied the Vipers. "The Phantom's men are searching for the vendor. We're going to give them a welcome they won't forget."

Big Tony asked, "Got a plan, Blake?"

Blake replied with a grin, "More than a plan, I've got a show."

As The Phantom's men reached the now-abandoned hot dog stand, Blake's voice called out, "Looking for something, boys?" Turning around, weapons drawn, they faced Blake. He taunted, "It's not polite to invade our territory uninvited."

A thug demanded the vendor's whereabouts. Blake laughed, "He's gone, but you're welcome to stay for the main event." The Vipers then emerged, surrounding The Phantom's men, setting the stage for a tense showdown.

The brutish thug growled. "You're making a big mistake, Hunter."

Blake's grin widened. "Am I? Because from where I'm standing, it looks like you're the ones in trouble."

The fight erupted in a burst of chaos. Blake moved with agility, using every available object as a weapon. He grabbed a discarded broomstick, swinging it like a sword. "On guard, gentlemen!" he shouted, knocking two thugs off their feet.

Buster joined the fray, lunging at a thug and grabbing his pant leg. The man yelped, trying to shake the dog off. "Help! This dog's a demon!"

Blake laughed, grabbing a trash can lid and using it as a shield. "Buster, surprise attack!" he called out, bashing another thug in the face with the lid.

One of The Phantom's men charged at Blake with a knife. Blake sidestepped gracefully, grabbing a nearby mop and thrusting it forward. "Cleanup on aisle five!" The thug stumbled, slipping on the soapy water that splashed onto the ground.

As the battle raged on, Blake's antics grew more outlandish. He grabbed a can of spray paint, shaking it vigorously. "Street art, special edition!" he declared, spraying a thug in the face which temporarily blinding him.

"I surrender, I surrender!" the thug cried, stumbling backward.

Blake's laughter echoed through the alley as he continued to dispatch The Phantom's men with humor and ruthlessness. He spotted a group of thugs trying to sneak up on him and grabbed a nearby fire extinguisher. "Time to cool things down!" he shouted, spraying them with a cloud of foam.

The Vipers fought alongside Blake, inspired by his daring and fearless approach. Together, they overwhelmed The Phantom's men, who were no match for their combined forces.

As the last of the thugs lay defeated, Blake stood victorious, breathing heavily but grinning from ear to ear. He approached one of The Phantom's men, who lay on the ground, barely conscious. Blake aimed his gun at the man's forehead and fired, the sound echoing through the alley.

"Adiós, amigo," Blake said with a smirk. "Viva la comedia del combate!"

The Vipers cheered; their spirits were lifted by the successful battle. Blake knew that this was just one victory in a long war, but it was a step in the right direction.

"Great job, Buster!" Blake said, ruffling the dog's fur. "Let's get out of here and take some rest before the next ambush.

As they made their way back to the hideout, Blake couldn't help but feel a sense of accomplishment. The fight had been a testament to his creativity and resilience, and it had shown The Phantom's men that he was not to be underestimated.

The war was far from over, but with each battle, Blake and Buster grew stronger. They would continue to fight, using every trick in the book, until justice was served.

The Vipers fortified their hideout, turning it into a makeshift fortress. Blake ensured that every corner was covered, every exit guarded. The anticipation was palpable, and the air was thick with tension.

As the clock struck midnight, the sound of approaching footsteps echoed through the darkened streets. Blake and the Vipers readied their weapons, knowing that this would be a battle for their lives.

The Phantom's men emerged from the shadows, their faces twisted with anger and determination. The leader of the group, a scary thug named Ripper, stepped forward with a wicked grin on his face. "Time to pay the piper,

Vipers."

Blake stepped out into the open, his eyes locked onto Ripper's. "Bring it on, you cowards."

The fight erupted in a whirlwind of violence. Blake moved with lethal precision, his strikes are calculative and brutal. The Vipers fought with a savage intensity, their survival instincts kicking in.

Blake grabbed a nearby crowbar, swinging it with bone-crushing force. The first thug crumpled to the ground, blood splattering the walls. "That's for thinking you could take us down!" Blake shouted.

Buster, ever the loyal companion, lunged at a thug and clamped his powerful jaws onto the man's arm. The thug screamed in agony, blood pouring from the wound as Buster shook his head violently.

The Vipers fought fiercely, their attacks are ruthless and unyielding. Big Tony wielded a massive wrench, bashing skulls with a sickening crunch. "You picked the wrong gang to mess with!" he roared.

Blake spotted Ripper advancing on him, a gleaming blade in hand. Ripper lunged at Blake, but Blake was ready. He sidestepped the attack, grabbing Ripper's wrist and twisting it with bone-snapping force. Ripper howled in pain, dropping the blade. Blake didn't hesitate. He delivered a series of brutal punches to Ripper's face, each strike fueled by a burning rage. "This is for every life you've taken, every friend you've hurt," Blake growled. "Just kidding, I don't give a damn" Blake whispered in his ear before, he took the blood covered pipe and...with a final, bone-crushing blow, Ripper fell to the ground, blood pooling around him.

The fight continued to rage on, the air thick with the scent of blood and sweat. Blake and Buster moved as a deadly unit, cutting down enemy after enemy with ruthless precision.

Blake grabbed a gasoline canister, pouring its contents across the floor. "Light it up!" he shouted to Tony.

Tony ignited a rag and tossed it onto the gasoline, setting the room ablaze. Flames roared to life, engulfing The Phantom's men in a fiery inferno. Their screams filled the air as they were consumed by the blaze.

Blake and the Vipers retreated to a safer distance, watching the hideout burn. The flames danced in Blake's eyes, a reflection of the unrelenting fire within him.

"We did it," Tony said, panting heavily. "We took them down."

Blake nodded; his expression resolute. "This is just the beginning. We won't stop until every last one of them is gone."

As the hideout burned to the ground, Blake and the Vipers knew that the war was far from over. They had won a brutal and bloody battle, but more challenges lay ahead.

With each victory, Blake and Buster grew stronger, more determined. They would continue to fight, using every ounce of their strength and cunning.

After the brutal battle, Blake and the Vipers gathered in their hideout, the air thick with the scent of victory and the lingering tension of the fight. Blake, still catching his breath, looked around at the gang members who had fought alongside him. He felt a sense of belonging he hadn't experienced in a long time.

Big Tony, noticing Blake's contemplative expression, clapped him on the back, his large hand warm and reassuring. "You did good out there, Blake. Real good."

Blake nodded, a small smile tugging at the corners of his mouth, though his eyes still held the weight of the recent battle. "Thanks, Tony. I finally feel like I've found a place where I belong."

As the adrenaline of the fight began to wear off, Blake was left with a flood of emotions. The scent of gasoline and smoke still lingered in the air, a stark reminder of the chaos they had just survived. He looked around at the faces of the Vipers—each one marked by the same exhaustion yet lit with the same flicker of triumph.

Blake's mind wandered back to the moment he had first joined the gang, like a heart broken man seeking solace in the only place left to him after the bomb attack that had shattered his world. The memory of the explosion, the sight of his family's lifeless bodies, still haunted his every step. Turning to the underworld seemed the only way to numb the pain, to find a semblance of purpose amid the ruins of his life.

The gang members gathered around, curious to hear more. Blake took a deep breath and began to share his story. "I wasn't always like this. I had a family, a job, a normal life. But everything changed when a bomb attack took away my parents and hospitalized my little brother. I was left with nothing, and I turned to the criminal underworld to survive and to support my brother, Jake"

The room fell silent as Blake continued. "I joined a gang, thinking it would give me a sense of purpose. But it only led to more pain and loss. I lost my brother, Jake, to violence. I became a mercenary, driven by revenge and the need to survive. But it never filled the void."

Blake's voice wavered, but he pressed on. "I thought I was alone, that I couldn't trust anyone but Buster. But then me and Buster found you guys. You fought by my side, and for the first time in a long while, I felt like I had a family again."

Big Tony stepped forward, "Blake, being in a gang has its pros and cons, but there's one thing we never do, and that's betray a member of our gang. Betrayal is the worst thing, and we never do it, even if it saves our lives. You can even kill us if you want to. We have done what you asked.

The other gang members nodded in agreement, their faces reflecting the same sentiment.

Tony continued, "You finish what you have started, Blake. Live your life as a mercenary or not, we don't give a damn. But know this: you're one of us now, and we'll stand by you no matter what."

Blake felt a surge of emotion, a mix of gratitude and determination. "Thank you, Tony. Thank you, everyone. I won't let you down."

The gang members cheered, their camaraderie and loyalty evident. Blake knew that the road ahead would be tough, but with the Vipers by his side, he felt ready to face whatever challenges came his way.

As the night wore on, the gang shared stories and laughter, the bond between them growing stronger. Blake looked at Buster, who was curled up contentedly by his side, and felt a sense of peace he hadn't known in years.

For the first time in a long while, Blake felt hopeful. He had found a family in the Vipers, and together, they would fight for justice and redemption. The war was far from over, but with each battle, they grew stronger, more united.

The Vipers and Blake had earned a brief respite after their victory, but there was no time to rest on their laurels. The air was thick with anticipation, and everyone knew that the war was far from over. However, the most unexpected turn of events was about to unfold.

In a dimly lit, smoke-filled room, the air heavy with the scent of cheap cigars and spilled whiskey, Aiden, a ruthless and cunning adversary, sat across from Goodman, a figure of power and influence. Both men shared a common enemy:

Blake Hunter.

"We're both losing men," Aiden growled, his eyes burning with fury. "Blake Hunter is a thorn in our side, and he won't stop until we're all dead or behind bars."

The Goodman nodded, his expression cold and calculating. "Agreed. If we continue to fight separately, he'll pick us off one by one. But together, we can crush him once and for all."

Aiden leaned back, his lips curling into a sinister smile. "So, an alliance, then? For now, at least."

The Goodman extended his hand, and Aiden shook it, sealing the unholy alliance. "Let's make sure Blake Hunter regrets the day he ever crossed us."

Meanwhile, Blake and the Vipers were preparing for the next phase of their plan. Blake stood before the gang; his expression was serious. "We've won a battle, but the war is far from over. We need to be ready for anything."

Big Tony nodded in agreement. "What's the next move, Blake?"

Before Blake could respond, Alex, their tech-savvy informant, burst into the room, with a look of urgency on his face. "Blake, you need to see this."

Alex led them to a laptop, where a live feed from a hacked security camera showed Aiden and The Goodman shaking hands. Blake's eyes widened in shock. "No way. They're teaming up?"

Alex nodded grimly. "It looks like it. We're in for the fight of our lives."

Blake's mind raced as he considered their options. "We need to prepare for the worst. They're going to come at us with everything they have."

The Vipers rallied, their resolve unshaken. They fortified their hideout, setting traps and preparing for the inevitable assault. The sound of metal clanging, the smell of gun oil, and the tension in the air were almost tangible. Blake knew that the upcoming battle would be their toughest yet, but he was determined to see it through.

As the Vipers worked tirelessly, Blake told the gang, "This is it, guys. The final showdown. We need to hit them hard and fast. No holding back."

Big Tony clapped Blake on the shoulder. "We've got your back, Blake. No matter what."

Blake nodded, a steely determination in his eyes. "Let's show them what we're made of."

As they moved through their hideout, the dim lighting cast long shadows, the flickering bulbs adding to the tense atmosphere. Blake couldn't help but smirk at the thought of the chaos they were about to unleash.

Blake's thoughts turned to Aiden and The Goodman. He knew why they were teaming up and they were desperate. Their operations were falling apart, and Blake was the common threat. "Desperation smells worse than those cheap guns you scoundrels have," he muttered, trying to lighten the mood.

Big Tony laughed, shaking his head. "You're one ruthless knave, Blake."

"Hey, it's called survival, Blake shot back with a wink.

The night wore on, and the tension was palpable. Blake knew that the final battle would be upon them soon. But with the Vipers by his side, he felt ready. "Alright, team," he said, his voice steady and resolute. "Let's go out there and show them what we're made of."

Big Tony raised his weapon, a determined look on his face. "For the Vipers!"

The rest of the gang echoed the sentiment, their voices strong and unified. Blake couldn't help but feel a surge of pride. They were ready for whatever came next. "Remember," he said with a smirk, "in the words of John McClane, 'Yippee-ki-yay...'"

V

TONY'S GAMBIT

The night of the final confrontation arrived, cloaked in darkness. The tension hung heavy in the air as the Vipers, fully armed and prepared, braced themselves for the imminent assault from Aiden and The Goodman's combined forces. Blake stood at the forefront, Buster by his side, his mind focused on the battle ahead.

Blake sauntered into the dark alleys, his leather jacket glinting in the scarce light. With a smirk plastered on his face, he locked eyes with his target and sneered, "Alright, sweetheart, time to tango. But just so we're clear, by dance I mean an all-out brawl where only one of us leaves breathing."

The sound of approaching footsteps echoed through the darkened streets, and the Vipers readied their weapons, knowing that this would be a fight to the death. Blake took a deep breath, his heart pounding in his chest. "Remember, we're in this together. Let's give them hell."

As the battle lines were drawn and the first shots rang out, Blake knew that this would be a fight unlike any other. The clash between the Vipers and the combined forces of

Aiden and The Goodman would determine the fate of all involved. The stakes were higher than ever, and the outcome remained uncertain.

With the flames of war igniting once more, the final showdown has begun.

The combined forces of Aiden and The Goodman emerged from the shadows, their faces twisted with anger and determination. The battle erupted in a whirlwind of violence, the clash of weapons and the screams of combatants filling the night.

Blake moved with lethal precision, his strikes calculated and brutal. He wielded a machete, slicing through his enemies with a ferocity born of desperation. Blood sprayed through the air, painting the ground in a gruesome tableau of carnage.

Buster, ever the loyal companion, lunged at Aiden's men, his powerful jaws clamping down on limbs and throats. The dog fought with a savage intensity, protecting Blake with every ounce of his strength.

Big Tony, wielding a massive sledgehammer, fought with a fury that matched Blake's. He swung the weapon with bone-crushing force, smashing skulls and shattering bones. The Vipers fought fiercely, their attacks ruthless and unyielding.

The alleyway where the battle raged was transformed into a scene of utter chaos. Shadows danced wildly as gunfire and explosions lit up the night. Blake and the Vipers used their environment to their advantage, turning dumpsters and abandoned vehicles into makeshift barricades.

Blake's movements were fluid and relentless. He ducked and weaved, avoiding bullets and knife strikes with uncanny agility. He spotted one of Aiden's lieutenants advancing on him, a wicked grin on his face.

The lieutenant lunged at Blake, but Blake was ready. He sidestepped the attack, grabbing the man's wrist and twisting it with bone-snapping force. The lieutenant howled in pain, dropping his weapon.

Blake didn't hesitate. He delivered a series of brutal punches to the lieutenant's face, each strike fueled by a burning rage. "This is for every life you've taken, every friend you've hurt," Blake growled.

With a final, bone-crushing blow, the lieutenant fell to the ground, blood pooling around him. Blake stood over him, breathing heavily, his eyes filled with fury.

The fight continued to rage on, the air thick with the scent of blood and sweat. Blake and Buster moved as a deadly unit, cutting down enemy after enemy with ruthless precision. But the odds were against them, and the Vipers continued to fall.

Blake grabbed a gasoline canister, pouring its contents across the alleyway. "Light it up!" he shouted to the remaining Vipers.

One of the Vipers ignited a rag and tossed it onto the gasoline, setting the alley ablaze. Flames roared to life, engulfing Aiden's men in a fiery inferno. Their screams filled the air as they were consumed by the blaze.

Blake and Buster retreated to a safer distance, watching the flames rise. The fire provided temporary respite, but they knew it wouldn't be enough to halt the onslaught.

Big Tony, bloodied but still fighting, joined Blake at his side. "They're relentless, Blake. We need a new plan."

Blake's mind raced as he assessed the situation. "We draw them into the buildings. Narrow spaces work to our advantage. Set traps, use every piece of cover."

The Vipers rallied, their resolve unshaken. They moved into the nearby buildings, setting traps and barricading doorways. The narrow corridors and rooms provided a perfect battleground for close-quarters combat.

Blake led the charge, using his knowledge of the terrain to outmaneuver and ambush their enemies. Each room became a deadly arena, with Blake and Buster taking down foes with brutal efficiency.

As the fight raged on, Blake couldn't shake the feeling that this was only the beginning. The combined forces of Aiden and The Goodman were vast and determined, and the battle was far from over and the outcome remained uncertain.

Blake met Aiden's attack head-on, their blades clashing with a shower of sparks. The two men fought with a ferocity that bordered on madness, each strike fueled by a burning desire for vengeance.

Aiden's blade sliced through Blake's arm, drawing a deep gash. Blood poured from the wound, but Blake didn't falter. He countered with a brutal strike to Aiden's ribs, the force of the blow sending Aiden staggering backward.

"You can't win, Aiden," Blake snarled, his voice filled with cold determination. "I'll kill every last one of you if I have to."

Aiden's eyes blazed with fury as he lunged at Blake again. The two men clashed in a whirlwind of steel and blood, their movements a deadly dance of violence.

Blake's strikes were relentless, each one aimed to maim and kill. He drove his machete into Aiden's shoulder, the blade sinking deep into flesh and bone. Aiden screamed in agony, but Blake showed no mercy. He twisted the blade, tearing through muscle and sinew.

Aiden's eyes widened in terror as he realized he was outmatched. "No... this can't be happening," he gasped, blood pouring from his wounds.

Blake's expression was cold and unyielding. "It's over, Aiden. You lose."

With a final, bone-crushing blow, Blake drove his machete into Aiden's chest. Blood sprayed across the room as Aiden's lifeless body crumpled to the ground.

Blake breathing heavily, his eyes filled with fury. The fight continued to rage on around him and he knew that the battle was far from over.

The Vipers fought valiantly, but their numbers were dwindling. One by one, they fell, their blood mingling with that of their enemies. The air was thick with the scent of death and the cries of the dying.

Blake knew that they couldn't hold out much longer. He needed to find a way to turn the tide of the battle, to give them a fighting chance.

As the first part of the final fight drew to a close, Blake and Buster prepared for the next wave of enemies. The night was filled with the sounds of war, and the outcome remained uncertain.

Suddenly, Blake heard the sound of a door closing behind him. He turned, his senses on high alert. "Our guy, the Goodman, is hiding," he muttered to himself.

Blake walked up to the door, his machete still dripping with blood. He kicked it open, revealing the Goodman cowering inside. "Hola," Blake said with a cold smile.

The Goodman's eyes widened in terror. "No, please! Don't kill me!"

Blake's smile faded, replaced by a steely determination. "You don't get to beg for mercy. Not after everything you've done."

With a swift, brutal motion, Blake drove his machete into Goodman's chest, the blade piercing his heart. Blood sprayed across the room as Goodman's lifeless body crumpled to the ground.

Blake gained the confidence to complete the task sooner than expected, but the fight continued around him, with madness on both sides due to their heavy losses.

The chaos of the battle had decimated all the gang members including the Vipers.

Only three were left alive, including Buster, Blake and Tony, both of whom were battered and on the verge of collapse.

They were surrounded by the destruction of their fallen comrades, and the weight of loss was suffocating. Blake's mind was a mess, trying to process the carnage, the faces of the people he'd lost. But it wasn't just the bodies that haunted him; it was the feeling that something was off, like a piece of the puzzle that didn't fit.

Blake, his bloodied hands clutching his side, leaned heavily against the wall as he tried to steady himself. Buster was barely standing beside him, struggling to stay upright. Their breathing was labored, and the reality of their situation was sinking in.

But then, a voice cut through the haze.

"Look around, Blake. Look at what you've done."

Blake's eyes shot toward the source of the voice, his heart hammering in his chest. It was Tony - Big Tony, his body slumped against a pile of debris, but his eyes were still sharp, filled with something Blake couldn't quite place.

Blake's head swam as Tony's words hit him, his legs shaking. "What the hell are you talking about, Tony?" he rasped. "We've fought through all this. We've won, we"

"Won?" Tony interrupted, his voice cold and venomous. "You think you've won? All this bloodshed, this war, was part of your plan from the beginning. Your plan."

Blake's stomach twisted. "What? No. I didn't plan any of this."

Tony smirked; his expression was dark. "No, you didn't plan it. But you *were* part of it. You thought you were taking down the Phantom, the Goodman... trying to build something. But you were just a pawn, Blake."

Blake's mind raced. "What are you saying? I've been fighting for the Vipers, for everyone!"

"You think that's what this was about?" Tony spat, his eyes narrowing in bitter amusement. "This war... it was never about the Vipers. It was about using you, using your rage. Your sense of purpose."

Blake stepped back, the truth of Tony's words seeping into his bones like ice. "No. You're lying."

Tony's laughter was sharp and hollow, slicing through the tension like a blade. "Lying? You still don't get it, do you? You were never the hero. You were the weapon - Jonathan's, Goodman's, and now the Vipers'. And the best part? You didn't even realize it."

Blake's heart pounded, and the world around him seemed to slow down. "Again, what the hell are you talking about?" He could barely stand, his breath coming in gasps.

Tony's eyes grew darker, more intense. "I knew everything from the start, Blake. The Phantom. Goodman. the bomb they set up years ago that killed your parents, I knew all.

They knew this day would come and they made you a mercenary, as a tool to do their bidding. They offered you power, and you took it.

But you didn't know the cost of it at that time. They used you to set the Vipers and the other gang against each other, knowing the destruction would come."

Blake's mind was spinning, a sick realization crawling up his spine. "No... no. I would never have"

Tony's voice grew even colder. "You didn't know, but you've been playing their game all along. And when you thought you were setting it all up, you were just doing what they wanted. You thought you were leading the charge against the Phantom and the Goodman, but they were the ones pulling the strings the entire time."

Blake's stomach churned. "And what does that have to do with Emily?" he whispered, knowing exactly where this was going.

Tony's eyes flashed with fury, his voice trembling with a mix of rage and grief. "Emily Tony... my daughter, she is the one who fought against the very thing you helped create. She was protesting against the terror you helped set in motion. She was trying to make a difference in this messed-up city... and you killed her for money."

Blake staggered, his legs nearly giving way as Tony's words struck like a hammer blow. His voice cracked, raw with desperation. "No... Tony, I swear, I didn't kill her. I'd stake my life on it - on my parents' memory."

Tony's sneer deepened, his face a mask of bitterness and triumph. "Of course, you didn't kill Emily. And you didn't kill Jonathan either," he said, his voice dripping with mockery. "But that's the thing, Blake. You didn't even know. The bomb - years ago? That wasn't just a random act of terror. It was Phantom, tying up loose ends, wiping out all the evidence you had against him. And you? You should've listened to your manager that day. You could've walked away, could've had a happy, quiet life. But no... you just had to play the hero."

Blake staggered slightly, his breath catching in his throat, but Tony wasn't done. His voice turned colder, sharper, cutting deep. "You've spent years fighting battles you didn't understand, chasing enemies you couldn't even name. You don't know who you're fighting for or what you're even fighting against. You think you're smart? Your dog - your *Buster,* has more sense than you. At least *he* knows his boss."

Blake's blood turned to ice, his heart pounding in his chest. Tony's words thundered over him, relentlessly.

"You didn't know we were the ones who pulled you into this. We lit the match, Blake. We made sure the fire spread. You? You're not a hero. You're nothing but a weapon - a dog trained to hunt. A loyal *Buster* for us. And every single time you thought you were striking a blow for justice, leading your men into battle, killing those people? You were doing exactly what we wanted. Playing right into the hands of the men you thought you were fighting against."

Blake's knees nearly gave out. His mind raced as he struggled to piece together the devastating truth. "You mean..." his voice faltered before rising in anger and despair. "All this time... it was you? You orchestrated everything? But why? To avenge Emily's death?"

Tony let out a cold, hollow laugh. "Avenge her?" he spat. His voice dropped to a low, menacing growl. "You still don't get it, do you? I didn't just *orchestrate* this, Blake. I *led* it. Every step of the way."

Blake staggered back, his world shattering around him. His entire life, everything he had believed in, fought for... was a lie!. And Tony, the man he had trusted, had used him, manipulated him to cause unimaginable pain. His mind reeled with questions. Was Jonathan alive? Would it be possible? How had he missed the signs?

Tony's eyes bore into Blake's with a chilling finality, "And now, everything ends here. I brought you here to die".

"Tony, please tell me where is Jonathan? Where is he hiding?" Blake's eyes search eagerly to complete the unfinished task.

Tony with a cruel smile, "Blake, it is better for you to take your questions to the grave, because they don't matter. None of these matters. You are just a toy in our play."

And with that, Tony's hand gripped the gun, and before Blake could react, a shot rang out.

Blake's world was dark, a suffocating blackness that seemed to swallow him whole. He wasn't sure how long he'd been unconscious. His mind was foggy, his body a battleground of pain and exhaustion.

But then, slowly, his senses began to return.

The first thing he felt was warmth a soft pressure against his side. He shifted, wincing at the pain that shot through his body, but it wasn't the kind of pain that made him want to scream. No, this was the pain of life, of still being alive. It took a moment for Blake to piece it together.

When his eyes fluttered open, he found himself lying on the cold, rough ground. The night sky above him was **thick** with clouds, and the remnants of battle seemed far away, distant. But there, beside him, was Buster his loyal dog, sitting with his head resting gently on Blake's chest.

Buster's eyes met his, a look of understanding in the dog's gaze, as though he knew the truth before Blake did.

Blake's chest heaved with a broken sigh. He could barely move, his body stiff and bruised, but the familiar presence of Buster was a comfort, a reminder of the life he'd once had. A life he could never go back to.

Buster nudged Blake's arm with his nose, the dog's usual playful energy replaced with something softer, something more caring.

Blake's chest tightened as his gaze fell on his loyal companion, the only constant in his fractured world. His voice cracked, barely audible against the oppressive silence. "Was it you, buddy? Did you save me from him? What... what happened to Tony?"

He strained to lift his head, his body screaming in protest. His eyes locked onto the crimson pool spreading beneath Big Tony, the man's neck still bleeding, the ground slick with his lifeblood. The sight was both a grim relief and a haunting reminder of the chaos that had unfolded.

Blake's eyes darted around the room, scanning for any sign of Tony's men. The weight of the moment pressed down on him, suffocating and inescapable. He forced a chuckle, though it was jagged and hollow, a desperate attempt to mask the fear clawing at his chest. "Guess I'm running out of time, huh, bub?" he murmured, his words heavy with resignation.

The air hung thick with tension, the silence broken only by the faint, rhythmic sound of his companion's breathing. Blake's mind raced, grappling with the gravity of what had just transpired and the uncertain road that lay ahead.

Buster's tail wagged slightly, but Blake could see the sadness in his eyes. There was a bond between them, a shared understanding that ran deeper than words.

"I thought I was the one who would change things, get vengeance." Blake murmured, the tears welling in his eyes as he looked up at the stars above. "I thought I was the one who'd fight for something better, for something real. But what am I? What side am I really on? I'm nothing but a monster."

His breath hitched. "I never thought I'd betray people like this. Never thought I'd become the very thing I swore I would fight against. But here I am. And they tried to kill me. And they did…"

He closed his eyes, taking in a ragged breath as a cold tear slid down his cheek. "I was the weapon, wasn't I? Just like Tony said. And I… I never even saw it. I didn't even see the truth until it was too late."

He took a long, shaky breath. His chest felt heavy, burdened by the weight of all the destruction, all the pain he'd caused.

Blake shifted his head sluggishly, his vision swimming in a haze of exhaustion. His gaze landed on Buster, curled up faithfully by his side, those unwavering, loyal eyes fixed on him. A pang of emotion struck Blake, a lifeline in the sea of chaos surrounding him. He swallowed hard, forcing down the lump rising in his throat, and whispered hoarsely, the words quivering as they escaped.

"I was asked to kill Emily… by someone I didn't know. The money—" he paused, the weight of it pressing on his chest, "it was too big to ignore. But there was something off… a trap I couldn't quite figure out back then. Even so, I turned it down. I said no. But now—" His voice cracked, and he clenched his fists, the frustration surging like a storm. "I can't shake it. Who wanted Emily to be gone? Why was I set up against Big Tony?"

Blake's mind spiraled into a labyrinth of fragmented memories, tangled threads leading in countless directions with no clear path forward. The room within his thoughts felt suffocating—a pitch-black void lined with strings, each pulling him toward a different, incomprehensible truth. His heart thundered, chasing answers that refused to take shape.

"There's... someone out there," he murmured, his voice a whisper choked with anguish. "A devil I never saw... never even knew was standing in my way. But who? Who... who..." His voice faltered into silence, lost in the gnawing void of uncertainty.

The pain surged anew, clawing through him with a force that nearly brought him to tears. Blake's body trembled under the weight of it all—loss, confusion, betrayal. And through it, Buster remained, a silent and steadfast companion in the face of a crushing, unbearable reality.

A long silence hung between them, broken only by the faint sounds of the world moving on around them. Blake's voice grew quieter, ragged with shame. Blake whispered, voice trembling, you are a good dog, I made you as a weapon, turned you into something you were never meant to be. And now... now you deserve better. A better life, a better owner." He closed his eyes, forcing the words out. "Hell, even a devil in hell would have treated you better than I did."

As his voice trailed off, the weight of his past actions seemed to consume him. Then, like a tidal wave crashing through, the memories surged forward, and Blake's vision blurred into the distant past.

Blake coughed weakly, his body fighting to hold on to whatever life was left inside of him. But even as the darkness crept back in, he knew there was no way out. Not anymore.

"Go on, Buster. Find someone who'll treat you right. Someone who won't use you. I...I've failed you. I've failed everyone..."

Buster nudged Blake's hand; the dog's whimper soft but filled with emotion.

Blake smiled weakly, though the smile didn't reach his eyes. "You're a good dog, Buster. You deserve better partner than me."

He pushed himself slowly into a sitting position, the world spinning around him. His legs were unsteady, and the effort to rise felt impossible. But Blake pushed through it, determined to put some distance between himself and the life he had known—the life that had led him to this point.

Blake stood, swaying as he looked down at Buster. "I've done enough. This is where it ends."

Buster looked up at him, his ears perked, his tail wagging hesitantly, as though he didn't understand.

But just as Blake started to walk, his legs gave out beneath him. He stumbled forward, barely catching himself before he collapsed entirely. His body was too weak to carry on. His strength had long since run out.

Before he could stop himself, he fell to the ground, his body crashing hard against the rough earth. Pain exploded through him, but it didn't matter anymore. The end was here.

And as Blake's vision began to darken again, the cold emptiness creeping over him, he felt Buster's warmth beside him. The dog had never left his side.

Buster pressed his head gently into Blake's chest, nudging him softly. His warmth was the last thing Blake felt as tears began to fall down his face.

He didn't care anymore. The pain, the regret, the battles, it all melted away as he lay there, in the dirt, with his loyal companion by his side.

Blake closed his eyes, his final breath shaking as he whispered, "I'm sorry, Buster. I never meant for any of this, I put you in danger too. Countless times. The three gangs have killed me together."

And in that moment, Buster snuggled closer to him, his body trembling slightly, as though he understood the grief that Blake had carried. He didn't leave. Not then. Not ever.

And as Blake's breath slowed, as life began to slip away from him, Buster remained by his side—his faithful friend, even in the end.

Blake's last tear fell as the darkness consumed him. And with that, his journey came to an end.

Blake's last moments were filled with remorse and the haunting realization of the role he had unknowingly played in the grand scheme of destruction. The night was still, a silence that seemed to echo the weight of his actions, the lives he had unknowingly altered.

The night felt darker, colder as though the world itself was mourning the loss of a man who had been both a villain and a tragic hero in his own right.

Blake's body lay motionless on the cold earth, a heavy silence descended around him. The wind whispered through the broken buildings nearby, the remnants of the final battle scattered around like the debris of shattered dreams.

Buster, still nestled beside Blake, refused to leave his side. His soft whimpers filled the air as the dog's eyes watched Blake with a sense of confusion and sorrow. The world around them seemed to hold its breath.

Yet, in this moment, with Buster curled up next to Blake, it remained unmoving, unwilling to leave the only family he had ever known. Even as the hours stretched on, as the cold of the night deepened, Buster stayed; his body pressed against Blake's, a silent vigil for the man who had been more than a master.

Blake had been his friend, his companion, and his protector. And Buster, in return, had been the one constant in Blake's life – a reminder of loyalty, something Blake had lost long ago.

Somewhere far off, a distant siren wailed, breaking the stillness of the night. But to Buster, it meant nothing. It was just another echo of a world that had never truly understood the bond he and Blake shared. The pain of watching Blake slip away from him had been unbearable, and yet, Buster remained.

As the light from the rising moon cast an eerie glow over the two of them, Buster's ears perked up slightly at the faintest rustle in the distance. His gaze shifted toward the horizon, but no one came. No allies. No enemies. No saviors. The world had moved on, leaving Blake and Buster in their final, isolated moment.

Blake's body was stiff, but Buster could feel the faint pulse of his former master's heart, weak and fragile. And now, only Buster remained to carry the memory of a man who had fought and fallen, who had tried to save the very city he had once hoped to destroy.

Buster's eyes softened as he nudged Blake's still form, as if begging him to wake up. But it was hopeless. Blake wasn't coming back. The fight was over.

Buster stood, his tail lowering as his eyes filled with something deeper—something even harder to understand. The dog paced in small circles around Blake's body, but he never left. He kept glancing back at his master, as if hoping for some sign of life, some flicker of the man he had once known. But the world was silent. And Blake, the man who had given him everything, was not making any movement.

Time seemed to stretch on, endless and cruel. Finally, Buster let out a mournful howl, a cry that seemed to carry all the sorrow, all the loss of the night.

Then, slowly, Buster turned and began to walk. His movements were slow, deliberate—each step weighed down by the loss of his friend, the one person who had always stood by him.

He walked beside Blake's body, never once looking back. The bond they had was too strong, too pure, for even death to sever. Buster knew that Blake was gone, but he couldn't bring himself to leave the place where he had last felt his master's warmth.

For a brief, fragile moment, it seemed as though Buster was walking away from the pain, from the loss, from everything that had happened. But then, in an instant, Buser sense something and hear a shaky whisper: "Buster..."

And with that, Buster paused.

He turned back; his eyes fixed on Blake's body one last time. It was as if the dog understood that there was no turning away from the truth – no matter how much it hurt. And yet, the pull of loyalty, the bond between man and dog, was too great to deny.

With a deep breath, Buster lowered his head and nuzzled Blake's hand one last time. As though to say goodbye.

And then, Buster began to walk again. His body was shaking, his heart heavy with grief, but his steps were sure. Blake had been his world, and now that world had shattered. Yet Buster, even in his sorrow, knew that life would go on, and he would carry the memory of his fallen friend with him for as long as he could.

As Buster moved away from the place where Blake had fallen, his head held low, a strange peace settled over him. The moonlight bathed the streets in an ethereal glow as the dog disappeared into the night, the echoes of his mournful howls lingering in the distance.

And Blake, lost in his regrets and mistakes, remained where he had fallen, his body abandoned in the cold embrace of death, waiting for the last breath of a man who had never found peace.

Busters body hurt, his mind clouded with sadness, but there was something deeper pulling him forward. He didn't know where he was going, but he couldn't stop. He had to keep moving.

Maybe, just maybe, I'll see him again, Buster thought, his paws dragging through the dirt. *In the afterlife... when the pain ends...*

The thought of joining Blake again, beyond the cruel grasp of this world, was the only thing that kept him going now. The bond they had was unbreakable, even by death. And though Buster didn't understand the mysteries of life and death, he believed, in the deepest part of his heart, that one day, he and Blake would be reunited.

As the night stretched on, the city growing darker with each passing minute, Buster looked toward the horizon. The moonlight bathed the streets in a soft glow, and for a brief moment, it felt as though Blake's presence was still there, watching over him.

Buster's steps grew slower as his exhaustion caught up to him, but he kept moving, determined not to look back. His heart was heavy with grief, but his soul was searching for something more—something beyond the pain, beyond the loss. Blake, his owner, was the only person he ever wanted to see.

But the world had not stopped moving. In the distance, the sounds of vehicles approached, a sign that the city was waking once more, unaware of the profound loss that had occurred in the shadows.

VI
FANGS OF LOYALTY

As dawn began to break, the first light of morning cast a soft glow over the scene. The once chaotic battleground was now eerily calm, the remnants of the night's turmoil scattered and lifeless. Among the ruins, Buster remained beside Blake, his loyalty unwavering even in the face of death.

As time passed, the world carried on, oblivious to the man who had fought so fiercely for so little. The city, always a place of violence and shadows, continued to turn. The streets would never be the same without Blake Hunter, but life had a cruel way of moving forward, no matter how much pain it caused.

Blake lay motionless on the ground, Buster stood beside him, barking frantically for help. Just then, the sound of a car approaching pierced the silence. Headlights cut through the darkness, illuminating the dire scene.

The car screeched to a halt, and a man jumped out, eyes widening in shock. "Oh my gosh!" he exclaimed, rushing towards Blake. He dropped to his knees beside Blake, assessing the situation quickly.

"Hold on," the man said calmly. "You'll be fine." He then turned to Buster, who was still barking, and gently patted the dog. "You did well. I am a doctor, and your friend is in good hands. Let's proceed to help your friend."

The doctor quickly went to work, his medical training kicking in. He checked Blake's pulse and noted it was weak and thready signs of hypovolemic shock due to blood loss. "We need to control the bleeding," he muttered to himself.

He reached into his medical bag and pulled out sterile gauze pads and a tourniquet. Buster watched intently as the doctor applied the tourniquet above the bleeding wound on Blake's leg to slow the blood flow. The doctor then packed the wound with hemostatic gauze, a special type of gauze that promotes rapid blood clotting.

"Okay, now we need to establish an IV line," the doctor said, retrieving an IV catheter and saline solution from his bag. He located a suitable vein in Blake's arm and expertly inserted the catheter, securing it with tape. He attached the saline drip to provide Blake with much-needed fluids and maintain his blood pressure.

Rechecking his pulse rate, the doctor quickly connected the oxygen mask to Blake, ensuring that he received adequate oxygen to support his vital organs.

"Let's check for any other injuries," the doctor said, carefully examining Blake from head to toe. He identified a pneumothorax—a collapsed lung—caused by a penetrating chest wound. "We need to perform a needle decompression," he explained, reaching for a large-bore needle.

With precision, the doctor inserted the needle into Blake's chest, releasing the trapped air and allowing his lung to re-expand. Blake's breathing stabilized slightly, but the doctor knew there was still work to be done.

He administered a dose of intravenous antibiotics to prevent infection and a painkiller to help Blake cope with the trauma. Throughout the entire process, Buster stayed close, his eyes never leaving Blake, his presence a source of comfort and hope.

Hours passed like minutes and finally, Blake began to stir. His eyes fluttered open, and he saw the doctor and Buster by his side. "You're safe now," the doctor said, relief in his voice. "Thanks to your amazing dog."

Blake's body felt like lead, each breath an exhausting effort, but he could feel the warmth of Buster's fur against his hand. His loyal companion was still there, standing guard and Balke could sense the pain in the dog's eyes. Buster had never left his side. That loyalty—through all the darkness, through all the violence—was something Blake could never repay. Not yet.

The doctor, still kneeling beside Blake, glanced up at the sky for a brief moment before turning his attention back to Blake. "You're lucky to be alive," he said quietly. "We got you in time, but you've lost a lot of blood. You're not out of the woods yet."

Blake's mind felt foggy, like he was swimming through a murky stream, but he forced himself to focus on the doctor's words. "Who... who are you?" Blake managed to rasp out, his voice barely above a whisper. "How did you... how did you find me?"

The doctor's face softened with an odd mix of concern and determination. "I'm Dr. Alex Carter. A friend of... someone you know. Someone who cares about you." His eyes flickered down at Buster, who was still standing vigil beside Blake. "I know what kind of man you are, Blake. Your reputation precedes you. But you're not alone anymore."

Blake's heart skipped a beat, a flash of confusion striking him. A friend? Who could that possibly be? He struggled to keep his eyes open, but the pain, the overwhelming exhaustion, was pulling him under.

Buster, as if sensing Blake's fading strength, nuzzled closer to him, his soft, wet nose pressing gently into Blake's palm. The action brought a small, pained smile to Blake's lips. He was still here. And that was all that mattered, wasn't it?

Dr. Carter, noticing Blake's struggling state, continued working with practiced precision. He spoke calmly, but urgency echoed in his voice. "We need to get you to a hospital, but I can't transport you myself. Stay with me, Blake. Just stay with me for a little longer. We're almost there."

Blake's breathing was shallow, but he tried to focus on the sound of the doctor's voice. His mind raced, even though his body felt like it was slipping away. A hospital? No. The dark figures from his past were still out there.

Suddenly, a chill crept through Blake's veins. "The... the others... they'll... they'll come for me," he muttered, his vision blurring. "They won't stop..."

Dr. Carter's expression hardened for a split second. "Don't worry about them. You're not alone anymore, Blake. You've got people who care about you—people who are going to make sure this ends the right way."

A strange sense of relief washed over Blake at the doctor's words. But it wasn't enough to quiet the doubts, the constant fear that the nightmare wasn't over. He'd escaped death, yes—but the world he'd lived in was still out there, lurking.

The distant sound of sirens began to pierce the night air, growing louder. Blake's heart raced, the pulse of adrenaline fighting the fog in his brain. "Help's coming, Blake," Dr. Carter said as he looked up at the approaching ambulance lights. "Hold on just a little longer."

Blake turned his head slowly, "You... you said... 'I'm not alone,'" Blake whispered, his voice trembling with exhaustion and a bitter laugh. "Well, guess what, doc... I've never felt more alone."

Dr. Carter gave him a reassuring pat on the shoulder. "That's the thing, Blake. You don't have to face this alone anymore. You might think you're still in the dark, but there's a light now. A way out."

Blake tried to say more, to ask about the people who were apparently on his side, but the words got caught in his throat as the world around him started to spin faster. He tried to hold on, but everything felt like it was slipping away.

Just as he thought he might lose consciousness completely, he felt Buster's warm body curl up next to him, his steady presence reminding Blake that not all was lost. Not yet.

And with that, Blake's eyes fluttered shut as the world around him faded to black.

Blake's wounds were starting to catch up with him, but he wasn't about to let a little blood loss stop his show. Buster, ever faithful, led the way, tail wagging like he knew something Blake didn't.

Blake drifted in and out of consciousness during his stay at the hospital, the sterile white walls around him blurring into the haze of his pain. Buster never left his side, his quiet, steady presence anchoring Blake to reality even as his mind spun with unanswered questions.

Dr. Carter, calm and methodical, focused solely on Blake's recovery. Every visit was short but purposeful, with the doctor checking his vitals, replacing IV drips, and monitoring the healing of his injuries. "You've come a long way, Blake," he remarked one day, adjusting Blake's oxygen mask. "But the road ahead isn't just about healing your body—it's about making sense of why you're here."

Blake said little in response. He spent most of his time staring at the ceiling or resting a hand on Buster's back, letting the silence fill the room. But deep down, his mind churned like a storm. He was piecing together fragments of his memory—Tony's betrayal, Emily's death, the strings that had pulled him into this nightmare.

It was during one of Dr. Carter's routine check-ups that Blake finally broke the silence. "Doc," he said, his voice gravelly, "I need to get out of here."

Dr. Carter frowned, carefully folding his arms. "Blake, you're still not strong enough to—"

"I don't have a choice," Blake interrupted, his voice raw but determined. "There's something I need to do. Something I need to face." He shifted slightly, wincing at the movement. "Tony's gone, but his house isn't. If there are answers anywhere, they're there."

The doctor sighed, glancing at Buster, who was watching Blake with those steadfast eyes. "This isn't about rushing to find answers, Blake. If you push too hard, you'll undo the progress we've made."

Blake's jaw clenched; his resolve unshaken. "Doc, I appreciate everything you've done, but this isn't just about me anymore. There's more at stake than you realize."

Dr. Carter studied him for a moment before finally nodding. "Alright. But if you're set on leaving, take it slow.

And don't make me regret helping you."

Blake gave him a faint, tired smile. "You won't."

The following morning, Blake discharged himself against medical advice. His body protested every movement as he dressed, but the fire in his chest burned brighter than the pain. With Buster at his side, he left the hospital and stepped out into the cold air. The world outside was the same, but Blake wasn't.

As they made their way through the city streets, his thoughts lingered on Big Tony's house. It wasn't just a place—it was a battleground of memories, of betrayal, of truths he had yet to uncover. The answers he needed were there. And no matter what is waiting for him there, he was ready to face it.

VII
THE UNLIKELY ALLIANCE

"Well, here we go again," Blake muttered to himself, hands resting on his gun, eyes scanning the farmhouse. "Another dead end. Another mystery. Another day where I get stabbed and almost die for no good reason. Classic Blake Hunter."

Suddenly, a voice cut through the night, smooth and sharp as a blade.

"Looking for someone, Mr. Hunter?"

Blake turned, recognizing the voice instantly. It's Ava, Big Tony's second daughter. A whole lot of attitude and even more firepower.

There she was, standing in the shadows, gun in hand, looking like she stepped out of a crime boss's wet dream. Perfect, just perfect.

Blake let out an exaggerated sigh and raised an eyebrow. "Well, well, if it isn't Tony's little princess herself. Got a whole 'bad girl' thing going on, huh? Real subtle." He glanced at the gun in her hand. "Oh, and look at you, packing heat. I must be so scared."

Ava didn't move an inch, her eyes narrowing as she kept the gun aimed directly at him. "Keep talking, Hunter. One more word, and I'll put you down faster than you can crack another stupid joke."

Blake shook his head in mock pity, holding his hands up in surrender. "Oh no. Please, don't shoot. I mean, wow, it's so intimidating when a teenager points a gun at a guy who looks like he's been through hell. You've got me shaking in my boots, kid. And it's just your below average pistol

Ava's fingers tightened around the trigger, but she didn't shoot. "I told you to shut up. You put my father into trouble, and I lost him because of you."

Blake tilted his head, "Firstly, I am not responsible for that and even I just escape from the hell". Second of all, is it a family tradition, as literally every single one of you always points a gun at me, which irritates the hell out of me, attagirl!"

"Listen, sweetheart, you know your daddy's dead and you have got no more protection. You think you can just go around playing with a gun like you're some kind of action movie hero?

Ava's eyes turned colder, but before she could react, Blake had already snapped the gun from her hand, faster than she could blink. The gun was now in his grasp, pointed directly at her.

"Respect your elders, kid, and tell me you're not afraid now, and I'll pop a bullet in your forehead with ease!" Blake said, his voice dripping with sarcasm. "And next time, try to be quicker on the draw. You never know when a ragged mercenary's gonna take your toys."

Ava stood there, a vein in her neck pulsing with anger. "You think you can just walk in here and kill me as well and make a mockery of everything we've built?"

Blake shrugged, keeping the gun steady. "I don't make the rules, sweetheart. I followed money all these days but right now I am looking for answers that I must know before I die. So, tell me where Jonathan is?" Ava's eyes twitched at the mention of Jonathan, but she didn't back down.

"You think he's just gonna show up, huh? He's not the man you think he is. And you're already in way over your head."

Blake tilted his head, a grin spreading across his face.

"Listen up, sunshine. I've been neck-deep in chaos more times than I can count - heck, I've died twice, and here I am, still rocking 'your' gun, not even sure if it's actually yours or just another souvenir. I thought I killed him years back, but it seems he is still alive for a reason."

Ava got enraged by this, and lunged at Blake, her eyes blazing with fury. But Blake was ready. He sidestepped her attack, using her momentum against her, and pinned her to the ground, the gun still in his hand.

"Calm down, princess," Blake said, his voice cold and steady. "You're not gonna win this fight."

Ava struggled beneath him, but Blake's grip was unyielding. "You think you're so tough," she spat. "But you're just a washed-up mercenary devoid of purpose."

Blake's eyes hardened. "Maybe. But that makes me dangerous. And you? You're just a kid playing with fire."

He pointed the gun directly at Ava, his grip steady. Ava's eyes flashed with defiance. "I'm not afraid," she said, her voice unwavering. "You'll need me if you want to find Jonathan."

Blake's expression didn't change as he pressed the gun against her forehead. "And why should I trust you?" he asked, his voice cold and menacing.

Ava swallowed hard, but she didn't back down. "Because I am the only one left in my family and am not ready to die today, I'll help you if you leave me."

Blake studied her for a moment, then slowly lowered the gun. "Fine," he said, his voice still laced with suspicion. "But if you try anything, I won't hesitate to finish what I started."

Ava nodded, her eyes never leaving his, "Deal."

"For your information," Blake smirked, twirling an imaginary mustache, "I didn't kill your sister Emily. But hey, someone wanted it to look that way. Plot twist, it was Detective Ramirez. Dude went rogue, probably under orders from some shadowy Big Bad. No, it wasn't the Phantom, he bit the bullet the same night. Which, by the way, makes this whole mystery as confusing as assembling IKEA furniture blindfolded.

Ava narrowed her eyes, arms crossed, every bit the skeptical teen detective. "And why exactly should I believe a single word coming out of your overly dramatic mouth?"

"Because," Blake deadpanned, leaning closer with the intensity of someone delivering a punchline, "I killed Ramirez for framing me with that murder. And before you start painting me as the big bad wolf, it wasn't revenge - more like quality control. Can't have people out there besmirching the Blake brand."

Ava's scowl faltered, just a little. "So, you're saying you're not part of this mess... but then who is? Where's Jonathan in all this? I have not seen Jonathan a week after Emily was killed. This whole thing screams conspiracy -Emily, Jonathan, even my dad, Tony." Her voice cracked slightly but regained its firmness, " I thought you had the answers.

Instead, you're looking for answers too, like searching for a needle in a haystack."

Blake shrugged with a lopsided grin. "Hey, give me a break, Teen Sherlock. I didn't sign up for this Lifetime movie drama. But I'm telling you there's a puppeteer pulling strings and Jonathan may know something about it, but when I find them, it's game over."

Blake now realized that Ava still did not know who killed Tony on that day. It is logical, considering there was no one alive on that day except Blake and Buster.

"Blake, I need you to understand something about Emily," she began, her words heavy with emotion. "She wasn't just my sister; she was a force of nature. She stood up for what was right, even when it put her in danger. And now... she's gone because of it. They took her from us because she refused to back down."

She paused, her gaze locking with his. "But Emily's fight isn't over. I won't let it be. I owe it to her to keep her voice alive, to make sure the world knows what she stood for. I need you to help me, Blake. Not just for her, but for everyone she fought for."

Blake smirked, the familiar sarcasm returning. "Oh great, a heartfelt moment. Cue the dramatic music and roll the credits. But seriously, I appreciate it. Now, let's get back to finding Jonathan and making sure this doesn't turn into a soap opera."

They made their way out of the farmhouse, Buster trotting alongside them. The night was dark, the moon casting long shadows on the empty streets. As they walked, Blake couldn't shake the feeling that they were being watched.

"Stay sharp," he muttered to Ava. "I've got a feeling Jonathan isn't going to make this easy for us."

Ava nodded, her grip tightening on the small knife she'd retrieved from her boot. "I wouldn't expect anything less."

She wasn't doing this for herself. She was doing it on behalf of her sister. She knew that Blake was someone she had to tolerate with, as she had no choice or else she would be shot to death.

Blake and Ava made their way through the labyrinth of the city, heading toward the lair of Big Tony's old allies. Buster walked alongside them, his keen eyes and nose on high alert. The night air was thick with tension, and Blake's mind raced with thoughts of their upcoming encounter.

Finally, they reached a warehouse on the outskirts of town where Jonathan was rumored to be hiding. Blake's eyes lit up with determination.

"Alright, Ava, let's do this." Blake nodded his head. "And oh! Stay away from Buster while fighting! All bite! No bark!"

Blake pushed the door open, his gun ready in his hand. The room was filled with smoke and the murmur of voices. Big Tony's old allies, a group of hardened criminals, looked up as they entered.

"Well, well, look who decided to drop by," one of them sneered, a burly man named Vito. "Blake Hunter and Tony's little princess."

Blake's eyes narrowed. "We're here for information about Jonathan. Where is he?"

Vito leaned back in his chair, a smirk playing on his lips. "Information doesn't come cheap, Hunter. We've got a little job that needs doing. You help us, and we'll help you."

Blake's grip tightened on his gun. "I don't have time for your games, Vito. Just give us the information."

Vito chuckled, shaking his head. "It's simple, really. We've got a rival gang causing us trouble. Take them out, and you'll get what you need."

Before Blake could respond, Buster growled, his eyes locked on Vito. The room fell silent as the dog's low, menacing rumble filled the air.

Blake couldn't help but smirk. "Looks like Buster's not a fan of your cologne, Vito. Can't say I blame him."

Vito's eyes flicked to the dog, a hint of unease in his expression. "Control your mutt, Hunter."

Blake's smirk widened. "Oh, he's not a mutt. He's a highly trained, very discerning judge of character. And right now, he's telling me you're full of it."

Vito's face darkened, but he kept his composure. "Do the job, Hunter. Then we'll talk."

Blake's face was contorted with anger. "Yeah, I'm gonna just kill you right here and now."

Before he could make a move, Ava stepped in front of him, her hand on his chest. "Blake, wait. We need their help. Think this through."

Blake's eyes blazed with fury. "Are you out of your mind, Ava? These guys are scum. We can't trust them."

Ava looked up at him, her eyes filled with determination. "I know it's not ideal, but we don't have a choice. If we want to find Jonathan, we need their information. We can do this."

Blake gritted his teeth, the sarcasm dripping from his voice. "Oh, fantastic. A little side mission to appease the local mob. Just what I always wanted."

Vito clapped his hands, a gleeful smile on his face. "That's the spirit, Hunter. Now, let's get to work."

Blake and Ava geared up for the job, their expressions grim. As they left the hideout, Blake turned to Ava, his voice laced with sarcasm. "You know, this is really shaping up to be a funny day, making deals with these thugs, I might even get a free meal out of it."

Ava rolled her eyes but couldn't hide a small smile. "Just focus, Blake. We need to get through this."

As they approached the entrance, Blake turned to Ava, his voice dripping with sarcasm. "Alright, kid. This is where the fun begins. Ready to dance?"

Ava gave a determined nod, her grip tightening on her knife. "Let's do this."

Blake kicked open the door, and they were met with a barrage of gunfire. The room erupted into chaos, bullets flying and bodies hitting the ground. Blake moved with the precision of a seasoned warrior, his every move calculated and deadly. Ava was right behind him, her knife flashing in the dim light as she took down opponents with swift efficiency.

In the midst of the chaos, Blake couldn't help but break the fourth wall, addressing an imaginary audience. "Ladies and gentlemen, welcome to tonight's feature presentation: 'Blake Hunter and the Great Crime Spree.' Please, enjoy the show."

Blake ducked behind a crate, reloading his gun. He glanced at Ava, who was fending off two attackers with impressive skill. Buster was by her side, growling and snapping at anyone who came too close.

Blake smirked; his voice filled with mock admiration. "Look at you, kid. Turning into a real action hero.."

Ava rolled her eyes but didn't lose focus. "Blake, we need to clear this room. Now."

Blake nodded, his expression turning serious. He sprang from his hiding spot, firing with deadly accuracy. One by one, the rival gang members fell, unable to match Blake's relentless assault.

As they fought, Blake's mind raced with thoughts of Jonathan. This was their chance to get the information they needed, and he wasn't going to let anything stand in their way.

Finally, the last of the rival gang members fell, and the warehouse was silent once more. Blake wiped the sweat from his brow, his breath coming in ragged gasps.

They returned to Big Tony's allies; the air was thick with tension. Vito's smug grin greeted them at the door.

Alright, Vito," he muttered to himself. "Let's see if your information is worth the bloodshed.

Impressive work, Hunter. I'll admit, I had my doubts.

Blake's eyes narrowed. "Start talking about the words I like to hear, Vito. I need whereabouts of Jonathan."

Vito leaned back in his chair, his expression turning serious. "Alright, listen up. After you took down The Phantom, some of his old members formed a new gang. They've been lying low, but they're dangerous. And guess what? Jonathan's is leading them now."

Blake's face darkened. "Why would Jonathan join them?"

Ava's face grew pale. "Jonathan's with them?"

Blake turned to Ava, his voice stern, If Jonathan's with them, it means they're even more dangerous. We've got to tread carefully."

Vito nodded. "Do you still remember a person named "Lincoln", a close ally of Jonathan back in those days?

Yes I knew, But Lincoln is not in this business nowadays and he lives a low life searching for his soul, by the way he was good friend of mine those days, Blake replied.

Yes, but I know for a fact that he is in constant contact with Jonathan, and I sniff that they have some secrets between them. I know nothing more about it, Vito was very careful about stopping there.

Thanks for the lead, but don't expect any favors next time, Blake said with a sharp edge to his tone. His piercing eyes wandered, making calculated glances at the people behind Vito, as if searching for something or someone.

Vito laughed, a cold, harsh sound. "Don't worry, Hunter. I'm sure our paths will cross again."

Oh, don't worry! You won't be alive when the paths cross again! Blake replied, with a solemn look on his face, chuckling out loud.

VIII

THE SALVATION

The moon hung low over the docks, casting long shadows on the desolate landscape. The air was thick with tension, and the distant sound of waves crashing against the shore added to the eerie atmosphere.

Inside the warehouse, the air was filled with the rough laughter and raucous banter of Jonathan's henchmen. They reveled in their temporary reprieve, their voices echoing through the dimly lit space. The sound of clinking bottles and shuffling cards painted a picture of momentary camaraderie. But that all changed in an instant.

The heavy doors of the warehouse creaked open, and the room fell silent. Jonathan stepped into the room, his presence commanding and fearsome. The laughter died down, replaced by a palpable sense of dread. One of the henchmen, oblivious to the sudden shift in atmosphere, glanced around in confusion.

"Why did everyone stop?" he muttered, his voice breaking the silence.

Without warning, Jonathan moved like a predator, pinning the unfortunate henchman against the wall with a swift, brutal motion. His hand gripped the man's throat, cutting off any further words. Jonathan's eyes burned with a cold, unrelenting fury.

"I'll cut off your damn head if you prefer to have fun," Jonathan hissed, his voice a menacing whisper. The henchman's face turned pale, and he struggled to nod, his eyes wide with terror.

Jonathan released his grip, and the henchman slumped to the ground, gasping for breath. Silence settled over the room once more as Jonathan walked through his men, his gaze sharp and unyielding. His presence was a dark cloud, suffocating and oppressive.

He stopped in front of one of his most trusted lieutenants, his voice is a low growl. "Where is Blake?"

The lieutenant hesitated, fear flashing in his eyes. He had promised Jonathan he would find Blake within a week, but the elusive mercenary had remained just out of reach. Jonathan's patience was thin, and his fury was a force of nature.

Jonathan's hand shot out, grabbing the lieutenant by the collar and pulling him close. He pressed a knife to the man's throat, the blade gleaming in the dim light. "I asked you where Blake is. I've been trying to kill him for years, and somehow, he still survives. Like a cockroach."

The lieutenant's voice trembled as he stammered out a response. "We're close, boss. We've got leads. It's just a matter of time."

Jonathan's grip tightened, and he leaned in closer, his voice dripping with venom. "Time is something you don't have. Find Blake, or I'll make sure you regret ever crossing me."

He released the lieutenant with a shove, and the man stumbled back, nodding frantically. Jonathan's rage was a palpable force, dark energy that fueled his every move. He had become a living nightmare, relentless and unforgiving.

The silence was heavy in the warehouse as Jonathan's henchmen resumed their tasks, now with a newfound urgency. Jonathan's threat lingered in the air like a dark cloud, pressing down on them. As he turned and walked away, the tension remained palpable, a constant reminder of his wrath.

Meanwhile, across town, Blake and Ava were knee-deep in their investigation. They had taken refuge in Blake's dimly lit apartment, papers and maps scattered across the table. The room was a chaotic mess of leads and dead ends, but Blake's keen mind was piecing it all together.

Blake leaned back in his chair, a smirk playing on his lips. "Alright, Ava, let's see what kind of wild goose chase we've got ourselves into this time."

Ava couldn't help but smile at Blake's sarcasm, despite the gravity of their situation. "So, what are you up to?"

"Alright, Ava, here's the plan," Blake said, a smirk playing on his lips. "We're catching the metro."

Ava raised an eyebrow, clearly skeptical. "The metro? Blake you must be crazy to go out in the crowd?"

Blake chuckled, his smirk widening as he saw Ava's expression. "Oh, you bet your sweet cape I'm crazy. But listen, it's not about what you *think* we're doing, it's about what we *need* to do." He leaned in, lowering his voice with a serious mock tone. "We catch the 5:00 AM train, confront our source, collect the information and quietly leave the train, reach our hiding place quickly."

He raised his hands in the air like he was presenting the grandest of schemes. "Trust me, Ava. It's gonna be legion - wait for it."

Ava crossed her arms, unimpressed. "So, let me get this straight. We're going to take the metro, find this Lincoln guy, talk to him quietly, and then what? Hope he spills details on Jonathan movements?"

Blake's expression turned mockingly serious. "Precisely. It's very simple, right?"

Ava sighed, shaking her head. "You're impossible, Blake. And what makes you think he'll just give up whatever you are looking for on Jonathan?"

Blake's eyes gleamed with mischief. "Oh, he'll talk. Trust me. The guy's got a weaker spine than a paperclip. And if he doesn't, well, there's always plan B - Buster."

At the mention of his name, Buster let out a playful bark, wagging his tail as if he understood every word.

Ava couldn't help but laugh. Alright, fine. Let's go catch a metro and hope your insane plan works.

The city's metro station was a bustling hub of activity, even in the early hours of the morning. Blake and Ava blended in with the crowd, their eyes scanning for any sign of Lincoln. The minutes ticked by, and finally, they spotted him - a scruffy-looking man with a nervous demeanor, boarding the 5 AM train at the very last minute.

Blake nudged Ava, "There he is, it's showtime."

They followed Lincoln onto the train, keeping a low profile until the doors closed. The train rumbled to life, and Blake wasted no time making his move. He approached Lincoln with a casual swagger, his voice dripping with sarcasm. "Well, well, well. If it isn't my old buddy, Lincoln. Fancy meeting you here."

Lincoln's eyes widened in shock, clearly caught off guard. "Blake? What are you doing here and why are you chasing me?"

Blake's grin turned predatory. "Oh, you know, just enjoying a leisurely morning commute. Now, let me make it very simple and plain, "Tell me where Jonathan is, you know I don't like lies"

Lincoln's face paled and he stammered, "I-I don't know what you're talking about, please don't put me in trouble"

Blake leaned in closer, his voice dangerously low. "Don't play dumb with me, Lincoln. You've got one chance to make this easy on yourself. Otherwise, my friend Buster here is going to have a little fun."

Buster growled on cue, his eyes locked on Lincoln. The man's resolve crumbled, and he quickly nodded. "Alright, alright! Jonathan's hiding out at an old factory near the docks. I swear, that's all I know!. But you are in danger now and by making this scene you are taking me in your path"

Blake's smile turned cold. "Good boy, Lincoln. Now, get off at the next stop and disappear. If I ever see your face again, I won't be so friendly."

Lincoln didn't need to be told twice. He scrambled off the train at the next station, disappearing into the crowd. Blake turned to Ava, his eyes twinkling with amusement. "See? Easy peasy. Now, let's go pay Jonathan a visit."

Ava couldn't help but smile at Blake's antics, despite the seriousness of their mission. "You're something else, Blake. Let's just hope this lead pans out."

Buster barked in agreement, and the trio set off towards the docks, ready for whatever awaited them.

Blake, Ava, and Buster arrived at the old factory near the docks, the place where Lincoln had claimed Jonathan was hiding. The factory loomed before them, a derelict monument to a forgotten era. The moon cast eerie shadows across its crumbling façade, and the air was thick with the scent of rust and decay.

Blake's frustration was palpable as they searched the empty building, finding no sign of Jonathan. The realization that Lincoln had lied hit Blake hard, and his temper flared.

"Unbelievable!" Blake shouted, kicking a nearby crate, which splintered under the force. "That spineless weasel sent us on a wild goose chase!"

Ava tried to calm him down, her voice was steady yet gentle. "Blake, we'll find him. We just need to regroup and come up with a new plan."

Blake spun around, his eyes blazing with anger. "Regroup? Ava, we don't have time to play nice! Jonathan is out there, and every second we waste gives him an advantage."

Ava crossed her arms, her expression firm but understanding. "I know you're angry, but losing your cool won't help. You need to stay focused."

Blake's jaw clenched, and he took a deep breath, trying to regain his composure. "Alright, fine. But we need a new lead, and fast. I'm going to find that damn Jonathan, and I'll make him pay!"

Ava hesitated for a moment before speaking, her voice low but steady. "Blake, I hope you don't plan on killing Jonathan. Now, he may be working for The Phantom, but for long time he was very loyal to my dad. I won't allow another murder in this city, which is against my sister's ideology. Also, I want to know who killed Emily?

Blake's eyes flicked to Ava, and he forced a smile, masking the tempest brewing inside him. "Don't worry, Ava. I'm not going to kill Jonathan," he said lightly, his voice steady, almost convincing. "You are right, maybe there's more to his story."

Her eyes met his, the pain in them unmistakable. "I don't care what it takes. I just want the truth. I have to have it."

Blake nodded, keeping his gaze averted as a pang of guilt tugged at him. He knew exactly what she wanted - a reunion, answers, closure. But the truth was, he didn't care about Jonathan's side of the story. Ava had no idea on the depths of his rage, the haunting images that played like a broken record in his mind. To Blake, Jonathan wasn't a source of answers - he was a mark, a target, the embodiment of betrayal. And Blake had no intention of letting him walk away from what he'd done.

"You're right," Blake said, his tone calm and measured. "We'll hear him out, see what he knows. But if he's lying..." He let the words hang in the air, leaving just enough ambiguity to keep Ava from probing further.

She gave him a small, hopeful nod. "That's all I ask. Just don't make this about revenge, Blake. Let's get to the truth. Together."

Buster let out a soft bark, as if echoing Ava's sentiment. Blake glanced down at his loyal companion and ruffled his fur, keeping his expression neutral. "Yeah, together," he muttered, the lie bitter on his tongue.

As Ava turned toward the exit, Blake's smile faded, his face hardening into cold resolve. He clenched his fists, his mind racing with thoughts of Jonathan. This wasn't about truth or closure—it was about retribution. Jonathan had stolen everything from him, and no amount of words could change that.

Buster trotted after Ava, his tail wagging, but Blake lingered for a moment, staring into the shadows of the empty factory. "You'll get your answers, Ava," he murmured under his breath, his voice dark and resolute. "But Jonathan's not walking away from this. Not this time."

Blake stood by the cracked window of the dimly lit safe house, the faint glow of the city lights reflecting off his tense expression. Ava sat across the room, her arms crossed, watching him with a mix of curiosity and suspicion. She could sense something had shifted in him—his usual cocky demeanor was laced with urgency.

"Ava," Blake began, his voice quieter than usual, but steady. "I need you to listen to me. Things are about to get messy, and I need you to find somewhere safe."

Ava frowned, her posture stiffening. "What are you talking about? I'm not going anywhere. We're in this together, remember?"

Blake turned to face her fully, his eyes hard yet tinged with softer concern. "I've made a lot of people mad in this city. Now I've got some unknown enemy out there, and if you stick with me, well... congratulations, you're officially on the 'target' list.'"

"I can handle myself, Blake," Ava shot back, her voice firm. "You're not scaring me into hiding."

"I'm not trying to scare you," Blake said, stepping closer. "But I need you alive, Ava. And you being with me makes you a target. It's not worth the risk."

Ava studied him, her expression softening but not relenting. "So, what's your plan, huh? You go off, get yourself killed, and leave me to figure things out on my own? That's not how this works, Blake."

Blake gave a faint, humorless chuckle, shaking his head. "I'm not planning on dying, Ava. But I've got a lead. Something I need to follow up on, alone."

"Where?" Ava demanded, standing now, her voice edged with frustration. "What lead?"

Blake hesitated, then forced a reassuring smile. "Don't worry about it. Trust me, I've got this. Jonathan will look for me, not you. You need to stay somewhere safe until I've figured this out."

Ava stepped closer, her voice dropping. "Blake, you don't have to do this alone."

Blake's eyes softened for a brief moment before his resolve hardened again. "Yes, I do. You want to help me? Stay alive. That's the only way we're going to win this."

Before Ava could protest, Blake turned to the door, giving Buster a quick pat on the head as the dog fell into step beside him. "I'll be back," he said over his shoulder, his tone almost casual. "Don't do anything stupid while I'm gone." The weight of their unspoken words hung heavy in the air, and Ava stood there, rooted in place, the cool breeze tugging at her jacket.

And with that, Blake melted into the early morning haze, his footsteps echoing briefly before fading into the stillness of the world waking up. The faint glow of the first light of dawn barely touched the edges of the city as he headed for the train and this time to the station.

The sound of his boots on the pavement became a distant memory, leaving her standing alone with the chaos of her thoughts. Every question she had, every fear she carried, seemed to crowd in on her all at once. She couldn't shake the gnawing worry that whatever Blake was about to do might pull them both into something darker than they were prepared for. But there was no turning back now. Not when she was this close to the truth.

The 5:00 AM metro rumbled into the station, its brakes screeching against the rails as the early morning commuters bustled to board. Lincoln sprinted toward the train, his breath ragged, eyes darting over his shoulder to make sure no one had followed. Every instinct screamed at him to move faster, but he kept his pace steady, trying not to draw attention. He reached the platform just as the doors began to close, his hand slamming against the cold metal to stop them. With a final, desperate push, he slipped inside.

The train jerked into motion, but the brief moment of relief was fleeting. When it reached the next station, Blake was standing at the platform's edge, his posture relaxed but his eyes sharp, scanning every face in the train's windows.

Lincoln's heart skipped a beat when their gazes locked through the glass. Blake's eyes didn't leave him. He had found him.

Blake didn't hurry; he didn't need to. Every step he took toward the train was slow and deliberate, his presence undeniable. He wanted Lincoln to feel the weight of every moment, to know there was nowhere to hide. The train doors hissed shut with a finality that rattled Lincoln, and as the carriage jolted to life, he saw Blake step onto the train.

There was no escaping this now.

Blake's eyes never wavered, locked onto Lincoln with a calm, unsettling focus. The moment the doors closed behind him, Blake's gaze met Lincoln's fully for the first time. Lincoln's breath caught in his throat. His face drained of color, and his stomach twisted into knots. It wasn't fear - at least not just fear - it was the undeniable, sinking realization that whatever had been left unsaid, whatever he had hoped would remain hidden, will now be exposed.

Blake didn't need to say a word. The silence between them was louder than any conversation could have been. He was here. And Lincoln had nowhere left to run.

"Morning, Lincoln," Blake said, his voice calm but laced with cold amusement. "Miss me?"

Lincoln's eyes darted around, searching for an escape, but there was none. He swallowed hard, his voice barely above a whisper. "Blake... look, man, I told you everything I knew"

Blake slid into the seat across from him, his smile colder than ice. "You mean the factory? Yeah, we checked it out. Nice touch, by the way. Really set the mood for a wild goose chase."

Lincoln flinched, his hands gripping the edge of his seat. "I swear, Blake, I—"

"Save it," Blake snapped, his smile fading as his voice dropped an octave.

"The only reason I didn't kill you the last time we met was because of my brother. You remember him, don't you? Of course, you do. How could you forget? He vouched for you when no one else would. He believed in you. He had this... ridiculous faith in people.

And what did you do with that trust? You led him into the wrong place, into something he should have never been part of. Because of you, he was killed - gunned down by Jonathan right in front of me.

Blake's voice cracked for a brief moment, but he forced it steady, the rage swelling back like a gathering storm.

"He wasn't just my brother. He was the only family I had left, the only person who could pull me out of the darkness. And because of you, Jack is dead. Tell me, what did it get him, huh?"

Blake took a step closer, his eyes burning with fury.

Lincoln shifted uncomfortably and his breathing uneven. "You think avenging your brother will bring him back? You think it'll make you feel better? Trust me, Blake, it won't. Nothing changes."

Blake leaned forward; his tone sharp enough to cut steel. "I'm not here to avenge anyone, Lincoln. I'm here because something bigger is going on. Jonathan manipulated Big Tony into coming after me, and you... you're part of it. So, start talking. Now."

Lincoln hesitated and his fear palpable. But the weight of Blake's words and the searing intensity of his gaze finally cracked him. "Alright, alright!" Lincoln hissed, glancing around to make sure no one else was listening. "You want the truth? Fine. But you're not gonna like it."

Blake's silence was the only response Lincoln needed.

"Jonathan," Lincoln began, his voice low and hurried, "he wasn't the mastermind you think he is. He was a pawn, a slave in Big Tony's shadow. Always living in fear, doing what he was told. But then Emily happened."

Blake's fists clenched at her name, but he said nothing, allowing Lincoln to continue.

"I was part of the Vipers gang for a few years," Lincoln admitted, his voice wavering. "And I saw how things went down. Big Tony was ready to leave the game - his daughter Emily convinced him. She hated violence. Said it wasn't worth it. And you know what? Big Tony actually listened to her and said he was done with violence."

Blake's heart pounded, but he kept his face neutral, letting the pieces fall into place.

Lincoln's voice dropped even lower. "But Jonathan... he was terrified. If Big Tony got out, he'd lose everything. No protection. No shadow to hide behind. And if that happened, you would've taken him out without even blinking. So, he did the only thing he could think of - he planned to take Emily out of the equation. He gave the contract to you, Blake. Wanted you to do it for him, to kill two birds with one stone. But you didn't."

Blake's jaw tightened as he hear about the big trap set for him.

"But Big Tony didn't know that your turned down the contract, Lincoln's voice was shaky, almost as if the words were choking him. When Emily was killed, Tony was made to believe it was you. He came back into the gang world, all fired up, bent on taking you and every other gang down. He wanted revenge for her. Jonathan was the kingpin of all this mess you've been suffering for, and when I knew that you were with the Vipers, I knew it was game over, but still, you've somehow managed to come back, just like a cockroach."

Lincoln paused, running a hand through his hair, his eyes haunted.

"It's been kept under wraps, a secret. I've never said a word because I'm terrified for my life. After what happened to my friend Jake, I carry that burden every day, always looking over my shoulder.

Jonathan blackmails me all these days and makes me do small things for him."

And one day, while he was taunting me, he let it slip, laughing like a madman. He asked me if I wanted to join you and Jake... in hell."

He swallowed hard, his voice barely a whisper. "Blake, I don't have the strength to stand up to Jonathan. I can't even show my anger in front of him."

Blake's blood boiled, his mind racing with every revelation. But Lincoln wasn't done.

"Blake," he said urgently, leaning closer, "Jonathan's not done. He's always one step ahead. And now, with Ava by your side? She becomes a target. He'll go after her to get to you."

Blake's entire body tensed, his hands gripping the edge of the seat as the train roared through the dark tunnels. "Where is he now?" he demanded, his voice deadly calm.

"I didn't lie about the factory," Lincoln said quickly. "He was there when I met him last week. And if I know Jonathan, he's already planning his next move. I feel Ava is in danger, you need to keep her safe. If you don't handle this, Tony's entire gang will come after you, convinced that you're the one responsible for what happened."

Blake's mind raced as Lincoln's words echoed in his head. He needed to get to the farmhouse - his gut told him Ava might already be in danger.

He stood up suddenly, his gaze locking onto Lincoln. "Don't worry. Jonathan will pay for what he's done. You can live in peace forever."

Lincoln shrugged; his expression was unreadable. "I'll believe it when I see it. But if you need help, I'm here."

Blake's fingers flew over his phone screen as he dialed Ava's number, his heart pounding in his chest. The seconds dragged on as the phone rang... and rang.

"Come on, Ava, pick up the damn phone," Blake muttered under his breath, his grip tightening around the device.

The call continued, and Blake's anxiety mounted with each passing second. "Ava, damn it... Pick up," he muttered, his voice rising slightly. Finally, after what felt like an eternity, she answered.

"Ava!" Blake's voice was sharp, filled with panic and urgency. "Listen to me. You need to get out. NOW."

There was a long pause before Ava's voice came through, shaky and confused. "Blake? What's going on? Why are you—"

"Don't argue with me. Jonathan... he's the one behind everything. He killed Emily. He's been playing you this whole time. Ava. You're in danger."

Ava's breath hitched, her voice trembling with disbelief. "What? No, that's... that can't be true. Jonathan would never—"

"Don't trust him!" Blake cut her off, his frustration boiling over. "He's dangerous, Ava! I don't care what you think. He's been manipulating everything and now he's coming after you. You need to leave, NOW."

Ava went silent for a moment, her breath ragged on the other end. Blake's voice softened but was no less urgent. "Ava, please. Don't wait. You have to run."

"But... Blake, I don't know what to do. I don't have anywhere to go. He... he was supposed to protect me."

"You need to trust me. If you stay, it's too late. I can't protect you from here. You have to go, Ava. Please."

Another long silence before she finally spoke, voice trembling. "I don't know... but... if he's really after me... I can't stay here."

"I will not letting him get to you. Just get out of there. You'll be okay. Just go." Blake's voice cracked slightly with the weight of his words.

Ava hesitated, but then Blake heard the shift in her breath, the reluctant decision made. "Okay. I'm going. But Blake... don't let him find me."

"I won't. I swear it. Just go, Ava. I'm right behind you."

Without another word, Blake strode toward the doors, Buster padding silently at his side. As the train screeched to a stop, he stepped out onto the platform, his mind already focused on one thing: getting to Ava before Jonathan.

The city stretched out before him, shrouded in the early morning light. Time was against him, but Blake was nothing if not relentless. He glanced down at Buster, the dog's unwavering loyalty reflected in his eyes.

"Come on, boy," Blake muttered, his voice steely with determination. "We've got work to do."

The farmhouse stood on the edge of nowhere, shrouded in thick darkness, the kind that swallowed all sound. Ava sat near the old wooden stairs, gripping a lantern with shaking hands. But fear gripped her like a vice as her eyes darted to every shadow.

Then she heard it - a faint creak of floorboards above her.

She froze, her breath hitching. The air shifted, a presence weighing down the stillness. Slowly, deliberately, heavy footsteps descended the stairs. And then he emerged - Jonathan, his face gaunt and hollow, his eyes gleaming with a predator's hunger. In his hand, the glint of a blade caught the dim light of the lantern.

"Ava," he said, his voice soft yet dripping with malice, "you shouldn't have come here. You've only made this harder on yourself."

Ava scrambled back, her pulse pounding in her ears. She glanced around for Blake, but the farmhouse was silent except for Jonathan's deliberate approach. "Stay back!" she shouted, her voice trembling.

Jonathan laughed, a sound as cold as the steel in his hand. "Are you expecting a dramatic entry of your newfound friend, Blake? No, he isn't here, It's just you and me now. And trust me, he'll find out what happens when people stand in my way."

He lunged, and Ava dodged just in time, the lantern slipping from her grasp and shattering on the floor. Flames flickered, briefly illuminating Jonathan's terrifying grin. Ava stumbled, but before she could get far, he grabbed her by the arm, forcing her against the wall.

"You should've stayed out of this," he hissed, raising the blade.

And then, the window shattered.

Blake crashed through in a blur of fury, rolling to his feet with his gun drawn. "Let her go!" he bellowed.

Jonathan spun, his sneer faltering for a split second. "Blake," he said, his tone mockingly calm, "just in time. Always playing the hero, aren't you?"

Blake didn't waste words. He charged forward, the gun in his hand crashing against Jonathan's blade, deflecting it as the two men collided. The room exploded into chaos as they fought, every punch and block resounding through the old farmhouse.

Ava scrambled out of the way, clutching her throbbing arm as she watched the battle unfold. Blake's rage was palpable, his movements fueled by a ferocity she'd never seen before. But Jonathan fought with a desperation born of knowing this was his last stand.

Blake drove Jonathan back, slamming him into the stairs. But before he could press his advantage, Jonathan struck low, sweeping Blake's legs out from under him. The gun slid across the floor, out of reach.

Jonathan stood over Blake, his blade poised to strike. "You've lost, Blake," he sneered. "You'll never stop what's coming."

But before he could deliver the fatal blow, a feral snarl erupted from the shadows. Buster launched at Jonathan, his teeth sinking into the man's arm. Jonathan screamed, dropping the blade as he stumbled back, flailing against the dog's unrelenting attack.

Blake seized the opening, lunging for the blade and gripping it tightly. In one swift motion, he disarmed Jonathan completely, slamming the man to the ground and pinning him there. Buster barked triumphantly; his stance protective as he guarded Ava.

Under the dim, flickering light of Big Tony's farmhouse, Blake stood over Jonathan, bloodied and defeated on the ground. Blake's chest heaved with exhaustion, the weight of years of betrayal and death pressing down on him like an anchor. Buster sat nearby, growling softly, his body tense, ready to lunge if needed.

Jonathan coughed, blood dripping from the corner of his mouth, but his eyes still burned with venom. His laughter came out ragged, but it was enough to make Blake's fists clench.

"This…" Jonathan croaked, gesturing weakly to the chaos around them, "this is just a fight, Blake. You won this battle, but the war? It's far from over."

Blake's jaw tightened. "Shut up."

Jonathan smirked despite his pain, his voice gaining strength from the sheer malice behind it. "You think killing me will end everything? You think you'll walk away from this… clean? You're dreaming, Hunter. Gangs like mine… like Tony's… they don't just disappear. They reform…they evolve…and every one of them will have one name on their hit list."

He leaned forward slightly, his grin twisted, "Yours."

Blake's eyes narrowed, his hands trembling with fury. "I'm not afraid of them."

"You should be," Jonathan sneered. "Because as long as you keep fighting, they'll keep coming and when they do… you'll be alone. Again."

The words cut deeper than Blake wanted to admit. The void inside him - the one he'd been trying to fill for years with vengeance and violence - roared louder than ever. Jonathan's laughter started again, weaker this time, but just as cruel.

Blake couldn't take it anymore. His hand shot forward, grabbing Jonathan by the collar. "You don't get to tell me how this end," he growled, his voice low and dangerous. "Not after everything you've done."

Jonathan opened his mouth to retort, but Blake didn't give him the chance. In one swift, final move, he plunged the knife he'd wrested from Jonathan earlier into his chest. Jonathan's eyes widened in shock, his laughter dying instantly as life drained from him and this time for sure.

Blake stared down at him, his face unreadable, his breaths coming in shallow bursts. "It ends here," he muttered, more to himself than to Jonathan.

The farmhouse fell silent, save for the faint crackling of the broken lantern and the sound of Blake's ragged breathing. He dropped the knife and stumbled back, leaning against the wall as reality settled over him.

Ava stepped forward hesitantly, her face pale but her gaze steady. "Blake..."

He didn't look at her. Instead, his gaze drifted to the ground, his voice heavy with exhaustion.

"All this time," he said quietly, his tone hollow, "I've been chasing ghosts. Trying to avenge them, trying to find some kind of justice in all this chaos."

He let out a bitter laugh. "Lincoln was right. I never got anything out of it. Just... more emptiness."

Ava knelt in front of him, her voice soft but firm. "You're wrong."

Blake's eyes finally met hers, confusion flickering across his face. "What?"

Ava's voice trembled as she stood in front of Blake, her words cutting through the tension that hung in the air. "You're wrong," she said again, her eyes shining with a mixture of grief and resolve. "You didn't just chase vengeance, Blake. You did what my sister Emily wanted."

Blake's gaze dropped to the ground, his fists clenched at his sides. But Ava didn't falter. She took a deep breath, gathering what little strength she had left, before continuing, "You ended this. These gangs, this cycle of violence... you broke it. You think you were just avenging Jake? You were saving everyone else from the same hell you went through. Do you know how many lives you've saved, Blake? How many families won't lose their sons, their daughters, the way you lost Jake? How many mothers won't have to bury their children, how many fathers won't have to explain to their kids why their siblings aren't coming home?"

Blake felt the weight of her words crash over him like a tidal wave—relentless, unforgiving. He tried to swallow the lump in his throat, but it refused to go away. His chest tightened, old wounds he thought had long been buried ripping open once more. Ava's face blurred before him, her voice a distant echo in his mind. Suddenly, the room felt too small, too suffocating.

He had spent so long convincing himself that the war he fought was for justice—for Jake, for the people he loved. But now, Ava was telling him he was wrong. The real battle had never been about vengeance.

It had been about something far more fragile.

Peace.

For those still left in the city.

Tears burned at the edges of his eyes, but he refused to let them fall. Not yet. He couldn't bring himself to grieve for the things he had done, for the price he had paid. But Ava's words - her quiet devastation - echoed in his mind, and for the first time in a long time, Blake wondered if he would ever be able to forgive himself.

She was right. He had broken the cycle.

But at what cost?

How could he ever find peace when the city he had fought for now stood in mourning, a silent testament to the sacrifices made in its name?

And yet, as Ava waited for his answer, Blake realized she had given him something—a truth that cut deep, one he could never undo.

Peace might never come for him.

But maybe - just maybe - it had come for the people who needed it most.

Ava stepped closer and her voice was gentle yet firm. "That's not vengeance, Blake. That's change. That's redemption. You didn't get what you thought you wanted... but you gave this city something it desperately needed."

Blake closed his eyes, letting her words settle. For the first time in years, the chaos in his mind quieted, replaced by something unfamiliar. Something almost like hope.

He nodded slowly, his voice barely above a whisper. "I'm done, Ava. With all of it. The gangs, the fighting... everything. I can't do this anymore."

Ava squeezed his arm reassuringly. "Then don't. Let it go, Blake. You've done enough."

Blake looked down at Buster, who was now sitting quietly, watching him as if in agreement with his words. He reached out and ran a hand through the dog's fur. "Yeah, buddy," he muttered. "It's time to move on."

As the first rays of dawn broke through the farmhouse windows, Blake stood, his resolve steady. He glanced at Jonathan's lifeless body one last time before turning to Ava. "Let's get out of here."

Ava nodded, a small smile breaking through her exhaustion. "Where do we go?"

Blake looked out at the horizon, a faint glimmer of light cutting through the darkness. "Someplace quiet," he said. "Someplace we can finally breathe."

And with that, Blake, Ava, and Buster walked away from the farmhouse, leaving behind the ghosts of their past. War was over in their life and for the first time in a long time, Blake felt the weight of his burdens start to lift.

As they walked down the dusty path, Ava felt a sense of calm wash over her. The night's events were still fresh in her mind, but for the first time, she believed in a future where they could find peace. The sun climbed higher, casting warm light on the dew-kissed grass, and for a moment, the world seemed to hold its breath in anticipation.

Blake took a deep breath, the cool morning air filling his lungs, and felt a newfound sense of determination. They moved forward, step by step, leaving the remnants of their past lives behind. The road ahead was uncertain, but together they could face whatever challenges awaited them.

As they reached the edge of the field, Blake turned to Ava, his expression resolute, "We'll find a new place, some place where we can start over... Build something good."

Ava nodded, her eyes shining with hope. "I believe in you Blake. We can do this."

Blake smiled, the weight of his burdens lifting just a little more. With Buster trotting faithfully beside them, they are ready to embrace the promise of a new beginning. The road was long, but for the first time, they felt they were truly on the path to redemption.

Then, as if remembering something, Blake turned to the invisible audience with a sly grin. "Oh, and for those of you who have been following this little saga," he said, his eyes twinkling with mischief, "have you ever felt that life is just one long, twisted story? Sometimes you're the hero, sometimes you're the villain, and sometimes you just need a good laugh to get through the mess."

He paused for a moment, considering his words, then continued with a chuckle, "If you've ever been stuck between hell and heaven, let me remind you that life is about the journey, not the destination. We have all encountered demons, and it is wise to change our paths to avoid them but sometimes facing it head on is the only way to find peace.

Ava glanced at Blake, a smile playing on her lips. "You always know how to lighten the mood, don't you?"

Blake shrugged, his grin widening. "Well, someone's got to keep things interesting."

As they resumed their long journey, the laughter and conversation between them grew more animated, a stark contrast to the silence that once enveloped them. The road stretched out before them, winding through the fields and forests, taking them further from the shadows of their past and a step closer to heaven on earth, a peaceful life.

He walked the fine line between salvation and damnation like a tightrope walker without a safety net, knowing that the memories of those masked faces would forever bind him to both worlds. After all, salvation was a journey, not a destination, and Blake was just glad he had Buster to keep him company through it all. At least Buster never judged his questionable life choices! But at least there won't be any more bloodshed in his life, unless Jonathan's allies are out for revenge.

Between hell and heaven, Blake had found his path after a long search. Though he sought redemption and a brighter future, the shadows of his past would always linger, like a stubborn stain on his favorite shirt. The lives he'd taken, the faces that haunted his dreams, were etched into his soul - like those embarrassing tattoos people get in their youth. No matter how hard he tried, Blake could never fully escape the darkness, because those memories had a way of sticking around like unwanted party guests.

New Beginning

The sun was barely rising, casting soft golden light across the small house on the outskirts of town. Blake leaned against the kitchen counter, sipping his coffee, his gaze lost in the quiet stillness of the morning. The world outside was waking up, and for the first time in a long while, Blake felt like he could breathe freely. He wasn't running anymore. He wasn't chasing ghosts.

Ava walked into the kitchen, her school bag slung over one shoulder, looking so much older than when he first met her. The weight of her past was still there, heavy in her eyes, but there was a quiet determination in her step, a lightness that hadn't been there before. She was going to high school today. It was something she had always wanted but never had the chance to pursue. Blake had made sure of it.

Blake's heart clenched as he saw her, not the girl haunted by her sister's death or the girl running from the chaos of her past, but a young woman taking a step into a future she deserved. A future she could build. He had promised her this.

"Ready?" Blake asked, his voice soft.

Ava smiled; her eyes bright with something Blake hadn't seen in her for a long time – its hope.

I think so, she nodded.

He stood, walking over to her and gently adjusting the bag strap on her shoulder. "You're gonna do great, Ava. You deserve this."

Ava looked up at him, her gaze unwavering. "I'm scared, Blake. I don't know if I can... you know, fit in. I don't know how to do this without—"

Blake placed a hand on her shoulder, his touch reassuring. "Ava, you don't need to know everything. You just need to take it one step at a time, and I'll be here with you, I promise."

Her eyes softened, and for a moment. The world hadn't gotten any easier for her, but Blake had given her a chance to carve out something new and that was more than he ever thought he'd be able to offer.

Ava nodded and her voice was steady but full of emotion. "You know, Blake, no matter what happened... your life isn't over. It's just started; you don't have to carry the past with you forever."

Her words hit him harder than any punch ever could. **It's just started.**

Blake blinked, his throat tightening as those words echoed in his mind. Ava was right. He didn't have to let his past define him. He don't have to keep running from the ghosts of his parents or Jake or the life he had left behind. He could still move forward. He could still change and live his life.

Ava smiled softly, before turning and heading for the door. Buster, ever loyal, trotted beside her, his tail wagging in that simple way he had, as if everything returns to normal in the world.

Blake stood there for a moment, watching them. His eyes followed Ava and Buster out the door, and for the first time in a long time, his mind wasn't filled with regret or anger. Instead, there was something else fragile, yet strong.

He stepped outside, taking a deep breath of the crisp air. Morning sun is little warmer now and everything felt... different. Like the world had shifted, just a little, and offered him a completely new chapter.

Buster ran up to him, wagging his tail and looking up at Blake with that innocent trusting eyes. Blake bent down to pet him, feeling the warmth of the fur against his hand. He ruffled Buster's head, then paused for a moment.

Jake and his parents.....

Their faces flashed in his mind....the calm life and love before it all came crashing down. Jake, his brother, who had been his anchor and his reason to fight for so long.

His chest tightened and the familiar ache was rising like a weight inside him. No matter how much time passed, he would never be free of them, not truly. But it is somewhat different now. He wasn't drowning in the memories. He could carry them with him. They would always be a part of him, but they didn't have to define his every step.

Blake's hand tightened on Buster's fur, and it nuzzled into him as if sensing his turmoil. Blake whispered, his voice thick with emotion, "They're still here, aren't they, buddy?"

Blake stood up, wiping his eyes quickly before anyone could see. Then, he turned and walked toward the nearby graveyard.

The cemetery was quiet, the wind rustling through the trees that bordered the stone paths. Blake moved with purpose, his steps slow but steady, as if each one was a moment of healing. He reached the small plot where his parents were buried.

The flowers he'd brought were fresh, a simple bouquet of lilies and daisies. He knelt down, placing them gently on the grave. His hand lingered on the cold stone, tracing the engraved names of his parents.

"I've done whatever I could," he whispered, his voice rough with unshed tears. "I couldn't save you, but I will save her. I promise..."

The wind whispered through the leaves, as if the world itself was listening. Blake closed his eyes, his heart heavy but full of something new... a fragile peace.

And then he felt Buster's warm body press against him, as if to remind him that life didn't end in grief. Blake chuckled softly, wiping a tear from his cheek.

"They're still here," he murmured, more to himself than anyone else.

The cemetery was peaceful. Blake stood up, his thoughts, once clouded by revenge and regret, seemed clearer. He was finally able to let go.

Blake turned away and heading back toward the life he is building, towards Eva and towards a future he thought he'd never have.

And as he walked away with Buster at his side, he whispered softly, "It's just started....."

As I take a few steps back and contemplate the story of Blake Hunter, I am struck by the gravity of his story. Blake is a character who embodies the laws of motion and the principles of human complexity.

Blake's dark humor, moral ambiguity, and quest for redemption are reminiscent of the profound mysteries of the universe. His imperfections make him a relatable and multi-dimensional character, akin to the intricate dance of celestial bodies in the cosmos.

In conclusion, the tale of Blake Hunter is a captivating exploration of human nature, driven by the fundamental principles of gravitational motion that resonate with the very essence of our existence, much like the universal laws that govern the stars.